CHAOTIC GOOD

LEE KLEIN

Sagging
Meniscus

Set in Minion with LaTeX.

ISBN: 978-1-952386-47-3 (paperback)
ISBN: 978-1-952386-48-0 (ebook)
Library of Congress Control Number: 2022941829

Sagging Meniscus Press
Montclair, New Jersey
saggingmeniscus.com

"... the flow of a good soul is always unimpeded ... the giver of names reviles everything that hinders or restrains the flowing of the things that are ... '*Blaberon*' ('harmful') means that which is harming (*blapton*) the flow (*rhoun*). *Blapton*, in turn, signifies wanting to grasp (*boulomenon haptien*). But grasping is the same as shackling, and the name-giver always finds fault with that."

—Socrates, per Plato's *Cratylus*

CHAOTIC GOOD

In 0, in an attempt to kill the infant Jesus Christ, Herod the Great, King of Judea, orders the execution of all male children under age two in and around Bethlehem, an atrocity eventually observed in England as the Fourth Day of Christmas, celebrated by beating children in their beds, and as the Day of the Holy Innocents in Spanish-speaking countries, the equivalent of April Fool's.

In 1612, Galileo observes Neptune for the first time yet mistakes it for a star.

In 1836, Spain recognizes Mexico's independence.

In 1846, Iowa becomes the 29th U.S. state.

In 1895, in Paris, the first paying audience watches a movie.

In 1902, the first professional indoor football game is played at Madison Square Garden in New York City (Philadelphia lost to Syracuse).

In 1908, 75,000+ people died after an earthquake and subsequent tsunami strikes Messina, Sicily.

In 1937, Maurice Ravel dies.

In 1945, Congress formally adopts the Pledge of Allegiance.

In 1948, Zigaboo Modeliste (drummer for The Meters) is born.

In 1973, President Richard Nixon signs the United States Endangered Species Act.

In 2004, Susan Sontag dies.

In 2015, Lemmy (of Hawkwind and Motörhead) dies.

In 2019, on the 1077th day of Trump's presidency, on what would have been Guy Debord's 88th birthday, a terrorist truck bomb kills 84 and wounds 150+ in Mogadishu, Somalia, and the world's preeminent nerdy silly good-natured virtuosic ecstatic psychedelic maximalist alinear improvisational "jam band" plays the first of their annual four-night New Year's run of concerts at Madison Square Garden in Manhattan.

"And then the storm of shit begins"

In my early teens on the front-porch rocker completing pre-requisite summer reading I envisioned an inexact aerial patriarchal force excreting a colossal turd upon my head or, more so, upon the head of a minuscule proxy attempting to protect itself with a cocktail umbrella. I'm sure the image derived from a cartoon coyote, outsmarted again by a roadrunner, taking cover from a descending ten-ton anvil. But it appeared out of nowhere, this anxiety daydream about the impending school year, expectation of challenges ahead at the so-called Prep School, the closest school to home but considered the best in the state and among the best in the country.

Something about attending what I had always been told was *the best* school in the area transformed it into a *beast*, uncertainty up ahead anthropomorphized into a defecating godhead. I was exposed, out there under the celestial shitstorm, nothing more than a flimsy assembly of toothpicks and crinkly paper for refuge. The sense of who I was, put another way, was unformed, and every experience, everything I affiliated myself with, bolstered the umbrella.

Umbrella bolster, it's everywhere as a teenager, you just hold out your hand and it comes to you. After pulling everything toward you for decades, absorbing much, discarding more, you've established some shelter. Chronic intensive immersion in art, music, books, movies, sports, interhu-

man interactions, et cetera, intertwine until they're insep-
arable from who you are, like application files opened and
distributed through your system over time, always running
in the background, ready whenever needed.

FIRST SET
QUALITY INN

Nearly thirty years ago (September 8-9, 1988), the first time at this cylindrical hotel, which seemed as destined for demolition then as it does now, I stayed with two friends from school, Gregg and Crow. We drank whatever alcohol we'd managed to score thanks to Gregg, who at seventeen was bearish, fully bearded, bespectacled, maybe half-Pakistani. There's a Wikipedia entry for his surname, an aristocratic clan on the Arabian Peninsula, Yemen, western India, successful businesses, diamond merchants, the family name yielding the word for "right" or "truth" in Arabic. A member of this family had immigrated to the United States at some point and then in the late-1980s a son wound up boarding at a prep school five miles southwest of Princeton where he developed an appreciation for the Grateful Dead and agreed to participate in an excursion forty-something miles southwest of the school to see the band in Philadelphia and stay two nights at the Quality Inn, where we arrived and had too much too fast before walking long, unkempt, outer-city, empty-lot blocks to FDR Park.

I now like to run from our place in South Philly near the dueling cheesesteakeries on East Passyunk Avenue down to and around FDR Park's 1.5-mile loop, passing its famous skateboard ramps under the elevated highway, a few hours before Eagles' home games when the park fills with barbecuing, football-tossing, inebriating fans. But twenty-nine years ago on a weekend in early September we knew if we poked around the eastern edge of the park we'd find a spontaneous bazaar named for the band's 1977 quasi-hit "Shakedown Street." Once there Crow procured and distributed tiny pieces of paper we held together like toasting *and away we go*, popped on our tongues, and held to the roofs of our mouths to dissolve.

The winding path along the park's eastern periphery across Broad from the now-nonexistent/demolished Spectrum became a super-sclerotic spine on which a street fair with tables and tents established itself, as makeshift and rambling as the band's history including recent emergence into MTV success and sold-out arenas and stadiums where it so often seemed like one in ten thousand had come for the show. The appearance of the band in town, back when they allowed camping in the lot and vicinity parks, attracted everyone interested in experiencing a traveling carnival and requisite related amusements of the mind in the form of compounds available from roving Bedouin-like American males, white but morphing into pirate cavemen, subcutaneously tanned, bearded, often dreadlocked, maybe wearing a tapestry fashioned into a skirt or Guatemalan shorts and ratty sneakers, moving through tourists and less outwardly obvious devotees, young ones like us, high schoolers, college kids, fresh faces endangering the scene, on the run twenty-plus years, a good ol' alternative reality where the laws didn't quite apply. Now I envision these emaciated tanned carney-like young gentlemen most likely from privileged families, like a later college friend who sold doses on tour and whose father was among the most prominent astrophysicists in the world, young men immersed in the part they're playing, individuality dissolved into something along the lines of hippie American aborigine group identity, wandering with purpose like when the band took off on extended improvisations, dazed yet alert, intoning into the ears of select passersby the availability of *doses, shrooms, X,* always those three in that order, a mantra chanted by pedestrian peddlers of psychoactives, essential participants in the ritual, dispersing seeds for psychic reforestation in the form of perforated centimeters of paper, imprinted maybe with a Superman or blue skeleton or some arcane and enticing symbol, purchased for four dollars each or a discounted bulk rate (three for $10).

Alcohol blurred the peripheries, made it easy to move like an athletic sixteen year old, drawn ahead by arrival at the one place we wanted to be. It had come within striking distance, we had made it there, two nights with a day between, lighting out for territories populated by writhing, unkempt, odoriferous masses, those who shared our affection for the band and its music, referred to its members by first name, mercurial, avuncular, mythic, at times downright Olympian omnipresences in our lives.

Cassette recordings we borrowed and dubbed at high speed, growing our collections of Maxell IIs, handwriting setlists each in our own way, experimenting along the spine of the glossy fold-up cardboard insert and the strip of tape on either side of the cassette itself, ensuring what we wrote didn't smudge, really taking care, displaying ever-growing archives in racks holding however many dozen tapes, or just tossing them in shoeboxes. The impulse to collect had transformed from baseball cards to these vestiges of performances deemed notable enough to enter into distribution, the sound degrading with each generation, at best encountering a soundboard that sounded like a CD, and what was to come in an hour or so would one day be passed around, appreciated as part of the late-'80s resurgence after Jerry's diabetic coma and recovery, the "Touch of Grey" video and influx of young fans like us, like me, with a little baby fat still in the cheeks and the love handles.

In the few pictures from the era I'm taller and thinner than I remember. I avoided cameras at the time, the years of pre-adolescent chubbiness lingering in my self-image. In one of the few pictures from when I was sixteen, my legs are long and knees almost knobby, my hair thick, brown, overlong to all sides, especially in front, swept up and to the left, the lowermost edge of my bangs singed golden by lighters held too long to bowls. I wasn't fully formed, of course, couldn't legally drive let alone drink, never mind the other stuff taking effect, early evening, September 8, 1988, FDR Park along Broad Street across from the stadiums (JFK and the Vet, like the Spectrum, also razed and replaced long ago), during a transaction with a middle-aged Black guy wearing an off-kilter Rasta wig. He seemed more like a local than a tour head, and he let us hit a monumental joint he held to our lips of something strong and good, most definitely something we wanted to own in reasonable quantity. He said it was Thai Stick, which I had only heard of in a Cheech and Chong movie ("it's tied to a stick, man"), and disappeared into the crowd with $25 in exchange for an eighth of an ounce.

We veered from the path to find a spot under a tree to inspect our purchase and savor some more before the show, not that we needed more, considering the opening edge of the zephyr from another dimension, a breeze from no traditional point on the compass, insinuating itself into our atmosphere.

Oh how we were stoked to smoke some more of that shit!

But then what?

No way!

Seriously?

Fellows, we've been had . . .

Seems like this super-primo exotic mega-ganja is *in all actuality* a stalk of celery coated in peanut butter, laced with oregano and tarragon, and then rolled in a baggie.

Inconspicuously completing the transaction, alert for the fuzz, we'd handed over the money, pocketed the baggie, and turned away as the guy melted into the shuffling long-hairs and tie-dyes. Instead of giving thanks and praise to Jah we thought about searching for the guy and politely asking for our money back. We thought about trying to sell it to someone. But how? We didn't have a super-strong sam-ple for enticement. So we chalked it up to idiot innocence, huddled with the patchouli horde crossing Broad Street, maintained physical contact with one another, bumped shoulders, pinched shirt sleeves, and short-strided our way into the venue.

Tickets ripped, my first show, *finally*, the energy of it, *my god*, inside the belly of this circular beast, the crowded looping concourse inside The Spectrum where I'd seen a tennis match (Connors vs. McEnroe) and a Sixers game or two (at my first game, fans could still smoke inside). Gregg and I were each a few inches over six foot so we could see over the crowd somewhat but Crow's line of sight was restricted to the backs of vibrating humanoids. I held onto the hood of Gregg's straw-smelling Baja as we shuffled toward our seats along the packed reverberating fluorescent hallway, sounds swirling in the air above and taking ghostly shape, not that I looked up. I looked over at Crow and it seemed like all the color had left his face. Seconds later he decided he had to leave but instead of discussing it with us and "leaving" the cacophonous reverberating concourse toward our seats and cover of darkness and soothing focal point of the stage, he pushed open a side door, a guard said *no return*, Crow said he understood, and he left.

Gregg and I had to decide what to do: let stoned drunk friend experience urban wilds alone while beginning to trip his face off in a way that doesn't bode well for the rest of the night, or forget about him for now and enjoy the show?

Cell phones, still at least ten years off, would've resolved the situation in an instant. We could've arranged spatiotemporal meet-up coordinates post-show but there was no way to maintain the tether at the time, other than flexing telepathic muscles. Did he have a hotel key? Did he know which room we were in? Did any of us know which room we were in? *Which floor?* Did we know how to get back to the room? To the hotel? How had we even made it to Philadelphia to the hotel to the park to the venue to this door that opened out into what? How would Crow survive, exposed to wolves descending once night fell? Or if not criminal element then total freaking raging freakout? What if he were arrested, wandering naked in a nasty part of town?

The good ol' Grateful Dead were in the building doing whatever they did before they took the stage.

Our good friend Crow was outside the building doing whatever he was doing now, ticket stub worthless, not even something he could miracle (gift) to some desperate optimist waving index finger in the air.

There was really no choice or so it seems thirty years later.

There was exasperation and then a sense of "are we really going to do this?" before we took off in search of him and soon enough found him like a cat up a non-existent tree and talked him down and then figured out what we'd do since our plans had met with the unforeseen circumstance of good friend succumbing to insistent and strenuous impulse to escape into open air as soon as possible.

A gas station convenience store populated by everyone else who'd entered and then escaped post-haste, or at least it felt that way, all overheard speech incomprehensible, no sidewalks, jutting concrete, uneven earth, broken glass, the Quality Inn's cylindrical protuberance our beacon as we negotiated blasted street to rented room, where at one point "LA Law" was on TV and it seemed unbelievable they were all saying *salamander* in court, an unlikely word in context.

I sat on the edge of the bed closest to the television set. I turned to Gregg, sitting up in the other bed. I said "salamander?" and he confirmed "salamander," his voice lower and distorted in a way that produced, somewhat like a burp, a stream of blue and green accompanying his weird pronunciation.

Crow may have been sitting in an easy chair in the room, smoking, drinking, trying to steady himself. I don't remember his presence there. I don't think we were mad at him for leaving or mad at ourselves for following him out. The experience now encompassing everything was more significant. It was meant to happen this way, I suppose we thought, minds wide-open to magical thinking.

I looked at my face in the bathroom mirror for what felt like an hour as my reflection streamed through translucent ribbons of blue, green, and yellow, cutting like the bowsprit of a ship across high seas. Irises eclipsed by pupils engorged, whatever I saw in the mirror was beautiful, no question, as I streamed toward a special destiny, nothing specific at the time other than a sense that everything would work out fine.

Thirty years later (July 21-22, 2018), after work and retrieval of child from pre-school on a Friday afternoon, we all went to the Penrose Diner across from that same oddly cylindrical hotel. I had reserved a room and so after dinner I kissed wife and child goodbye and crossed the street alone. In the lobby, a woman who seemed French or Australian eyed my plasticky CVS bags filled with iced coffee, seltzer, gum, and sneakers. I also had a backpack and a laptop bag. I sort of said "you like my luggage?" Something about her made me think she didn't speak English but then she spoke, quietly in an accent I couldn't place, to the desk attendant, a pale Russian prematurely balding, who pulled hair forward from atop his head to create something like a thin line of bangs, almost always sort of smiling, the way a deranged cat almost always sort of smiles. The woman said they only had two towels for four people in the room. The desk attendant seemed to almost sort of smile and said you didn't have to come tell me, next time call, and then it was my turn.

I asked how many floors the hotel had.

He said fifteen.

I said I'd like a room on the highest floor possible, please, especially since the elevator is out and I don't plan to leave until tomorrow for dinner. It's really no problem to walk up fifteen flights.

He said people want rooms on lower floors, because elevator is out highest floor operative now is ninth.

I said I'd like a room on the ninth floor, please, ideally facing the city.

He looked on his computer and said I give you nice room, good room on ninth floor, I think 902 is good.

After I paid and had my keycard I started up the winding carpeted stairwell to the second floor, assuming the unclean carpeted steps would look like that all the way up, but once I reached the second floor the carpeted winding stairwell led to ripped carpets, stained walls, and the entrance to a poorly lit, gray, smoke-smelling stairwell that I ascended, the steps at one point sticky from a spill of some sort, probably soda but possibly blood. I paused after about five or six floors, feeling a little weak, but soon reached the ninth floor. I opened the door to a winding circular hallway, the floor curving forever in a way really only suitable for horror movies. I took a time-lapsed video as I walked once around the block, the defunct elevators and stairwell in the middle, sixteen rooms on the periphery, all doors a putrid orange beige, the circularity and low ceiling making it seem like the deck of a doomed submarine spaceship.

My keycard didn't open the lock the first few tries. I almost panicked about having to descend all those stairs but, right as I started to worry, the door opened to my "nice" room. Unlike the pictures online there was no comfortable sitting chair, something that had made me think I could use the hotel in the first place. I'd pictured sitting in the easy chair, writing for hours at a time. Otherwise, there was a rattling air-conditioner, two beds, a TV, a desk in front of a large window, a simple desk chair, no mini-fridge for the iced coffees I'd brought.

I moved the desk and angled it so when I sat behind it I'd face the beds. I wet a small towel and wiped the desk and put my laptop there and plugged it in. I arranged my drinks and gum in front of the TV and then sat down at the desk, adjusted the chair, and tried to write, distracted by a dramatic sunset over a stereotypical picture-perfect image of polluting industry, smokestacks emitting billowing white smoke, the unreal city complexity of whatever goes on there, all the little lights and flames, the infinite right-angled metallic connections like an elaborate construction set.

I deleted the first few lines I wrote and then remembered I wanted to try voice transcription so I read about how to turn it on and sat leaning over my laptop talking about the time I stayed in this same weirdly cylindrical hotel thirty years ago and what it's like now, but then when I reviewed the dictated text there were so many errors and oddities it resisted comprehension, the textual equivalent of a chair made of water.

I wrote five hundred words, a start to work on tomorrow, and then I turned out the lights after cranking the white noise app on my phone to drown out a woman complaining about something, a voice that seemed to come from just outside the window, as though she were airborne, and then I heard other voices, bangs whenever someone opened or closed the stairwell doors or shut their own door, and then later in the night I woke to hear the occupants of the room next to mine having sex. I turned the white noise down, imagining the scene just a few feet from my head on the other side of the wall, and then I cranked the white noise app and somehow turned off my alarm at 5:30 but woke again at 6:00 to drink a room-temperature black coffee and get to work, sitting in bed, glued to the keyboard, a book about Lithuanian Jews rebelling against the Nazis during WWII between my crotch and the warm underside of the laptop.

The Avengers, about young charismatic Jews resisting Nazi oppression and liquidation, seemed like an extreme guidebook, an experience to reference in case the current political situation devolved. I've always imagined the empty acreage intended for shipments of new cars toward the southeastern edge of the city near the Walt Whitman Bridge repurposed into internment camps for whichever group opposed the group in power. Paved lots breached by plant growth, already surrounded by tall chain-link fences, wouldn't be too difficult to reinforce and run some barbed wire across the top.

Sparking Oy

Before the December 28, 2019 show at the Garden, the last time I saw the band was June 29, 2019 in Camden, the night before I mopped floors and cleaned windows and packed our bulbous aerodynamic midsize hatchback with a final load to take to the new house, including all the cleaning supplies this time. It took a month of Wednesday and weekend visits to empty and clean the old place after two trucks hauled our shit to a hilly leafy enclave fifteen miles west where we acquired a new place that had dropped to our range after a year on the market and appealed to us despite apparently repelling everyone else. Train tracks behind it, wall-to-wall carpeting, floral wallpaper, musty basement, outdated bathrooms and kitchen, the opposite of an open floor plan—we could see what this hundred-year-old house could be in time, and with a six-year-old daughter, the highly ranked school system was a plus, as well as the path across the street that led a quarter mile through woods along a creek to a swim club we'd join.

In the city the previous summer we spent so many weekend afternoons at community pools and the nature preserve by the airport, the first step toward departure, although we didn't move for proximity to nature and private pools of water. Mamou's commute was killing her. Two hours each way. Her interim upper management position had transformed into an interview that lasted almost a year, the future uncertain, always being evaluated, unsure what the higher ups, all white men, thought of her. If I were in her position I would've externalized tension and freaked or just stormed out. It's a test of character, I said while cooking dinner, coaching her to keep it cool, admiring her ability to do so. The stress at work plus daily commute and time away from child with special needs contributed to the move more than nature and idyllic pools of water. But reducing commute and increasing proximity to child and nature first required considerable time, energy, and expense.

Empty and clean, the morning after I saw the band at the riverfront amphitheater in Camden on June 29, 2019, our South Philly rowhome seemed restored, the way it was when we first saw it in March 2011, but only after emptying and scrubbing the house other than the back of the basement where I'd played music and now stored assorted nonessentials we'd move later. Sticky goo accumulated over eight years I noticed and dealt with, all over the floors bits of goo unseen in the clutter and clash of daily life, all of it visible now. The more I looked at the floor the more every irregular grain in the wood resembled accumulated goo that might yield to Clorox wipes and the little brush I used. It's not like we never swept and mopped but we hadn't done so on hands and knees with nothing in the room to distract from the cleaning act.

My burden was twenty-five boxes of accumulated cultural artifacts. A box of books and records for every year since college seemed reasonable but it was daunting to see stacked in one spot. Ten boxes were precious, inscribed

with an encircled A in marker so I knew to privilege contents when unpacking, which hadn't really started in the
new house. First I had to finish the old house, sanitize it,
change toilet seats, capture dust bunnies.

I slept on an air mattress in Kali's former room, second floor street-side, phone emitting a custom blend of
pleasant soporific noise (meditation bowl, electric fan, bab-
bling brook). As the handover date neared I was relieved to
spend time in a clean empty house, ideally tidied, phone
streaming to portable speaker John Martyn's "Solid Air"
album on repeat, accompanied only by a backpack and
clothes I'd wear to work in the morning, fit from running in
April and May before the move, making use of early sunrise
to cruise at pace east to the river as the sky over Camden
brightened. Since moving in early June, engaged in active
physical labor, I simply felt good as I walked the neighborhood strip after I'd cleaned enough to earn some beers at
the bars I'd miss, saying goodbye after more than a dozen
years there.

It had changed so much and improved without a doubt.
Things that hadn't been things were things now. Storefronts empty since the 1980s occupied and alive, revitalized,
a destination, not yet annoying or overdone. On warm
clear June evenings the one-way northeastward diagonal
strip through South Philly's NSWE grid surged with foot
traffic and packed sidewalk seating at restaurants, but it's
not like we still went to restaurants that often. Before Kali
was born we had and then when we could bring her in a car
seat or stroller but other than a few noisy spots it wasn't ap-

propriate now that she sat at the table on her tablet, liable to disturb others, but more so we just for the most part preferred to make dinner and eat at home.

Because it might help me avoid my grandfather and father's fate I had been sticking to something like a time-restricted modified Mediterranean diet, felt so much better, bought jeans in sizes I'd never owned before, saw myself re-emerge from what had been something like a fat suit, always able to run and walk forever, just burdened with extra weight, eating Subway sandwiches with chips and Diet Coke for lunch too often, oatmeal for breakfast with a banana, pasta- and rice-based meals for dinner, heating frozen pizzas when too exhausted to bother, always selecting fries when we made it to the nearby pub we treated as an extension of our home, drinking beer whenever of course, a few here and there, nothing excessive.

My health had improved the previous year, the summer after Trump's inauguration. I ran well through spring and summer, lost twenty or thirty pounds, felt better, for the most part ate vegetarian, selected vegan options at the pub like the falafel sandwich, feeling virtuous, but that fall and winter I found myself addicted to the candy machine at work, hitting it up for M&Ms, Twix, KitKats, whatever chocolatey candy was available, $1.25 each, knowing something was wrong, eating them against my better judgment, self-sabotaging, saying aloud *I will avoid the fucking candy machine* and then going right to it and buying something and using the change on Lifesavers I'd eat four at a time until they were gone.

I considered contacting Human Resources and demanding they remove the vending machine and not have sugar and salt so readily available. The machine's upper-half offerings were all salt and the lower half all sugar and chocolate. I had to create a PowerPoint for a brief presentation about my achievements in 2017 and my goals for 2018, and I listed my greatest challenge in 2017 and primary goal in 2018 as *overcoming the candy machine*, presenting an image I found online of a vending machine cleaved and burned as though it'd been struck by lightning.

But then a few months into 2018, my weight approaching the highest it's ever been despite lifting, running on treadmills, and walking to and from work 3.5 miles, every day exceeding 10K steps per the pedometer on my phone, I heard a colleague talking about how he'd lost so much weight so fast. He'd started at the company in the summer, seemed sloppy and thick, but then one day I didn't quite recognize him down the hall. He worked in a different department, often remotely, so I didn't see him every day. The changes when I did see him, when I noticed him, therefore, were dramatic. He started to look svelte, elfin, wearing form-fitting clothes. He told me what he was doing, gave me the URL of the site he used with all the info, I looked at it, started it the next day, and within weeks I'd effortlessly lost twenty pounds. But the most miraculous thing, the absolutely incredible thing I wanted to tell everyone about: I no longer found myself attracted to the vending machine.

I stood in front of it and just looked at the M&Ms and had no interest. I no longer considered it food. I also started not eating until lunch at least, often later, effortlessly abstaining since I was still full and satisfied from dinner. I listened to hundreds of related podcast episodes as I ran and as I walked to and from work, read articles and clinical studies about nutrition and fasting, performing casual urgent research into the potential conservation of my cognitive abilities.

I was nine when my parents hired caterers after my mother graduated from college, the first and only time I remember them throwing a party. The second she saw me, one of the caterers, a middle-aged Black woman, said "*damn*, you HUSKY!" and I ran outside, ashamed and teary, thinking of myself thereafter as *husky*, always sort of scheming to lose weight, other than a few eras in my life mildly dissatisfied with how I looked and felt because my self-conception differed from what I saw in the mirror. Thirty-five years later, however, self- and mirror images were matching up.

I scheduled a checkup on election day, the 2018 midterms, as a goal on the horizon to work toward, and when that day came I voted and then went to the doctor, my weight down sixty pounds since my last visit less than a year ago, my blood pressure for the first time under 120/80 (it was always slightly elevated), my heart rate in the forties after walking a mile to the doctor's office, generally feeling triumphant, but then the subsequent blood tests revealed very high LDL cholesterol and my doctor wanted to put me on a statin. She suggested I avoid red meat and eat more "heart-healthy" grains and use canola oil instead of the coconut oil I had been using, entirely avoiding grains in favor of local grass-fed steak, organic chicken, fish, eggs, and spinach. My triglycerides were very low (a very good indicator), my HDL was high (a very good indicator), the ratio of the two suggested I would live forever, but because my LDL was high my doctor wanted to put me on medication for the rest of my life, a medication with potential metabolic complications that could lead to diabetes. I also had not much of a family history of heart disease but on both sides had diabetes and also wanted to avoid my father's recent development of Alzheimer's disease, which may be a metabolic disease, like diabetes, in which the brain cannot access enough energy.

My brain had felt foggier, I had been anxious and reactive, prone to angry outburst, during the vending machine era, but once I conquered it the anxiety dial seemed turned down, the hum that had always been there dropped to nothing, and I started to see the world through the lens of insulin sensitivity versus insulin resistance. Of all the oppositional binary dualistic pairs (red versus blue states, e.g.), I began to believe that the most significant and impactful *yet least considered* was insulin sensitivity versus insulin resistance. It wasn't a matter of fat versus thin but how we process the food we eat. So much of what's available to eat, nearly everything, is processed crap that spikes insulin our bodies have trouble regulating, plus we eat all the time, never letting our bodies rest except when asleep, so insulin is always elevated and we're always trying and eventually failing to lower it, we become insulin resistant, excess calories consumed in the form of carbs and fat overload storage capacities, we become more anxious, depressed, reactive, impulsive, controlled by addiction to sugar, flour, and processed seed oils in a way that we think is *who we are.*

We write it off as how we've always been. "Oh my blood pressure has always been a little high" I'd say at the doctor's office, same as I've always said I ran and drank beer to reduce anxiety, a preferable alternative to pharmacologic intervention. Anxiety developed in my twenties, right when youthful insulin sensitivity evolves into insulin resistance before it becomes, if chronically unregulated, prediabetes, then diabetes, cardiovascular disease, cognitive decline, possibly even cancer.

The country's political atmosphere I started to see as a symptom of generalized insulin resistance, which made me feel like a vampire or someone living in some alternate reality, seeing this nutritionally discombobulated version of the Matrix, saddened at the supermarket glancing at carts filled with processed carbohydrates, sugar, flour, and oil. I wanted to take strangers on a tour of the aisles. But then I kept seeing the thing that had healed me demonized for cruelty and environmental impact. I tried to buy most of the steak we ate from a woman-owned butcher in South Philly that only sold grass-fed meat from nearby farms. It was more expensive but the quality was obviously better, and the eggs they sold there had orange yolks instead of yellow, which apparently had ten times the omega 3s. On and on.

But the doctor's prescription made me doubt everything I was doing to a degree. What if it were really killing me? What if all the people I listened to and read online were charlatans, even though they were mostly doctors or in two cases engineers who deeply studied everything and were fit and healthy and you could hear in their voices were sincere and driven, and also for the most part weren't trying to sell anything.

I made a bet with my doctor: I would get a coronary artery calcification scan to determine my coronary calcium score and if elevated (>0) I would go on a low-dose statin. The scan took minutes, cost about $100, and revealed a score of zero, which meant I had a <1% of developing heart disease and having a cardiovascular event over the next decade. I wouldn't need to take a daily medication with possible side effects and deal with pharmacy refills and the psychological stigma of having somehow become a middle-aged dude taking medication to reduce the risk of heart attack and stroke.

I cut out coconut oil and ate more fish and chicken than steak, reducing saturated fat, and began to gain some weight, but it was early 2019 and we spent our weekends hibernating through winter, at most driving to the nature preserve, walking around a little, and then visiting a nearby Ruby Tuesday's.

We knew the servers there. It smelled a little like the bathrooms and cleaning supplies but it was comfortable and became something Kali demanded and Mamou and I enjoyed, this little ritual of taking the highway over the industrial swamplands near the airport, turning off toward the nature preserve, parking, letting Kali walk without fear of cars or stray hypodermic needles. More space, a different color field, grays and browns and yellows in winter instead of muted brick and salt-stained pavement and mashed newspaper mulch on filthy cement.

But there was a side thought: how do we work all week away from home and emerge on weekends only to drive to a nature preserve surrounded by toxic swamplands followed by lunch at Ruby Tuesday's, followed by a drive through the Navy Yard on the way home, along the river and then looping through a quiet corporate park, stopping whenever we saw deer so Kali could say hello, like a little urban safari experience, how has life come to this? There must be something more than this, there's gotta be something more. I suppose I always expected more, had experienced more, but only technology or television slows our rambunctious hyperactive kid who otherwise rampages through our lives, usually in a way we love and cherish and all the attendant joys of parenthood, but also drains us of the ability to do much more than duck and cover as we restore after the work week, exposed to her for two consecutive weekend days.

Kali had consistent trouble with kindergarten teachers and administrators exposed to her from morning until mid-afternoon five days in a row. She ran from classrooms ("eloped"), never followed directions, her special education director calling every afternoon with feedback. Consistent slight distress of near-daily calls most likely contributed in part to what wore us down to the point that in March 2019 we looked at houses between the city and where Mamou works, just exploring at first, just driving by an intriguing old farm house with a yard and pool, across the street from a huge wild park, directly along Mamou's commute, that looked like paradise online but once we drove by there was no way we would move there. It was on a busy road, the property was surrounded on three sides by developments, the house itself seemed smaller than in pictures. Zero interest living off the city grid, so many curves and hills, I started to feel sick.

We drove around in the same direction a few weekends later and looked at open houses, something to do, a little excursion, no real sense we're intending to move, at least not in my mind, same as when I looked at open houses the same time of year, late winter/early spring, with the woman I'd eventually refer to as Mamou, not that many months after we'd met, just something to do, no sense we were in the market to buy, and then months later we lived together in a renovated rowhome we owned in South Philly and six months later were married and seven months later Mamou was pregnant with Kali et cetera.

Unconscious or unintentional or unacknowledged propulsion felt more like fate than freewill. We were caught in the forward flow of life more than deliberating and deciding, submissive to an emerging interdependent duo that would soon expand into a trio. It felt right and natural, exciting and effortless, despite considerable effort to make it happen. I'd been sitting on the banks of a rushing river, living life on my own terms, slowly, meditatively, irresponsibly, wastefully, independently, wonderfully, mindlessly, but then plunged into the water, there's no alternative but to surrender to the flow.

In early 2019 as we looked at houses, just looking, no stated plans, it didn't occur to me we were repeating the process, this time with child, driving around as I sat in the passenger seat with a physical aversion to the winding hilly roads, the unfamiliar topography, plus the night before I'd eaten a gummy and drank some beers watching the local professional basketball team and felt off the next day, shoulders hunched in the car, glaring metallic light, each house worse than the next, impossible to imagine living there, irritated about using our time to once again drive around these winding hilly roads, feeling off the path, driving around Philadelphia's western suburbs toward Delaware again, wishing I were back in my little bachelor pad near the dueling cheesesteak places in South Philly, $510 rent, small but cozy, third floor in the middle of a block overlooking a park used for soccer and softball.

But then we descended along some railroad tracks into a wooded area without sidewalks, with houses set back from a narrow, raggedly defined road, with huge wild trees, and then we took a right onto a more settled road also without sidewalks. The houses were older and unique but not showy, half-hidden by unruly rhododendrons, embedded in nature, carving out some space in what seemed like a vital, ever-encroaching forest.

This is nice, I said, feeling my body relax, saying I could live on this road.

It was a beautiful wooded street with some sizable old houses and others more like what I imagine served the Shire in the Tolkien books, little stone homes with slate roofs and dense shrubbery and trees everywhere hanging with vines.

We stopped in front of a house with two huge trees, oaks maybe, and an enormous front porch. It seemed too large and like it'd be too expensive but we were just looking and it's an open house so why not?

I laughed and said I could live here, sure, of course, obviously, although it seemed completely impossible that we would ever be able to live on a street like this, in a house like this, with two huge trees out front like this, one for me and one for Mamou.

Inside it was like walking through the dormitories at the old prep school I'd attended for high school, the same type of rug in the narrow hallway, the same aged plaster texture of the walls, but with wall-to-wall carpeting and elaborate old floral wallpaper in the living and dining rooms, low ceilings, everything last updated in the early 1980s but in good shape, the carpeting thick and fresh in the living room with the fireplace, the second floor a maze of rooms each with multiple entrances, and the third floor unfurnished with hardwood floors, one room giving off to two smaller rooms. I would use the room on the right as my office. Mamou would use the room on the left with the '70s-style Tot Finder sticker on one of the small old settling windows, these rooms with angular ceilings thanks to the eaves.

It was immediately imaginable, living there, so much more room than our rowhome, seventeen feet wide, overwhelmed with Mamou's attempts to overcome the lack of an entryway closet. I had once suggested we always try to keep the space along the stairway clear. We should feature the side view of the stairway. It was wooden and clean and white and beautiful when sitting anywhere in the front room. But after eight years a view of the stairway was blocked. There was a salvaged dresser toward the foot of the stairs by the entrance, a heavy wooden piece of shit with heavy drawers in which we stored linens and whatever else, and on the second floor, Mamou's nook outside the back bedroom had become cramped with excess shelving, the problem always that she had too much stuff, not that she needed more shelving, but then she'd acquire more organizational elements to contain her excess, increasing clutter and reducing available space, forcing me to shimmy between a shelving unit along the wall and a waist-high six-foot-long dresser-type unit that reduced the second-floor corridor to only a few feet, completely impeding the all-important sense of flow. Instead of maintaining the general sense of flow, Mamou's instinct over time was to impede it. I had no say in the matter of course. She did it against her better judgment, a symptom of ADHD inherited from her Thai mother, nature and nurture teaming up to impede the second-floor hallway flow, the entryway flow.

Her apartment had been like that when I first went there, boxes everywhere even though she'd moved in months before, total nonsense once my eyes acclimated: random boxes with nothing much in each one, unclear if it was intended to leave the apartment with donations or recycling or trash or be unpacked in the bedroom or bathroom or kitchen or main room. After a few weeks I freaked on her boxes, consolidated contents, stacked them, moved from obvious paths. I did so with swiftness, without deliberation, intuitively charged to set her house in order, action that activated in this woman a sense that I could be the man for her, husband and father, who could order her disorder, who could intuitively and swiftly rationalize her life.

I had never considered myself neat or organized but neatness and organization had evolved as I matured. It snuck up on me by my mid-thirties, arriving without overt intention as a consequence of work, of understanding the importance of efficiency, minimizing unnecessary steps for example by creating a pyramid of shortcuts on my computer desktop to the projects I worked on, a sloped pyramid along the lower right margin of the screen, with each shortcut's placement prioritized so the projects closest to completion were at the top of the rightward-leaning pyramid while the base included fundamental shortcuts to rationally and efficiently organized folders on the server, folders that, once created to contain all the varied files saved for my department, would never require reorganization because they were specific and general, like for example past, present, and future subfolders in the overall projects folder. Once I organized the random files inherited from the previous manager of the projects I worked on, I never had to reorganize. The system of shortcuts on my desktop, the sloping pyramidal shape with the prioritized projects toward the top, made it so I wasted no extraneous thought or experienced agitation or annoyance as I clicked through levels of the server and instead zapped to exactly what I needed. Over time this system limited agitation and annoyance, every day, multiple times per day, an accretion of efficiency that let me enter a flow state and make progress as the hours passed.

Organization removes impediments to flow. It allows for effortlessness, a variety of mindlessness, attentive, active, automatonic efficiency, consistent effort achieved without trying, with minimal friction, all obstacles, no matter how minor, minimized in advance.

At work I was an individual contributor, essentially an editorial project manager. I could with consistent application of effortless attention push as many projects toward completion as possible, maximize efficiency and production, doing so out of a native respect for work, trusting that the better I work the faster the day will go, the more my employment will be secure and I'll be in good standing with colleagues around the world and the authors and editors we work with and I'll benefit financially as a result but also preserve autonomy and flexibility, maintain a moral right to cut out to watch Kali when she's sick or there's snow or whatever comes up here and there.

Everything's driven by anxiety in a positive way, a survival mechanism inherited most likely from my father's side, otherwise ignorant of Judaism at this point other than genetically ingrained preparation against the threat of persecution. It's less about fear than a desire for a clear conscience, anticipating potential issues and attending to them or raising them, not cutting corners, working consistently instead of slacking and trying to catch up, ensuring clarity of communications, bulleted lists, short bursts of text, reminders, pleasant respectful follow-ups, doing whatever it takes to achieve perfect employee-hood without being annoying about it, in part to maintain employment but also not to worry about grooming and dressing well. That drives me too. Wearing jeans and sneakers, streaming music all day through high-def headphones. From our city place I walked to work and back while I read if the weather accommodated, and that was something I wanted to protect but ever since the move I take the train and register a fall-off in well-being but not complaining because Mamou's commute is now only forty minutes by car. A member of the family, things aren't always optimized in my favor. Obstacles to flow sometimes help others. Level-headed boy, ya better bend.

Once the rowhome was cleared out and cleaned, the night before the afternoon I'd meet the tenants to hand over the keys after a quick walk-through, I attended an outdoor concert at an amphitheater across the river in Camden. It's difficult to describe how much had been accomplished, how much had been done, how many objects, some precious, some functional, most inessential, had been packed and conveyed to our new place or Goodwill or the municipal dumping grounds. How many pounds hefted in May and June? The enormity of it is an embarrassment. How could two adults and a child have so much stuff? More so, we were in no way extraordinary. Each with clothes and prized possessions and sentimental knickknacks, it was harrowing to think of the tonnage, staggering to consider the multiplicity and magnitude, the burden, the money and time spent acquiring it, the byproduct of a culture of consumerist entertainment, as though larding the home with cheap unnecessary crap imported from the other side of the planet had a moral dimension.

I had curtailed spending for two years to pay off loans taken at the start of graduate school in 2004, loans I took in excess of tuition and expenses to pay off credit card debt accrued when I'd lived in Brooklyn and quit a good job to write the summer before 9/11 vanquished employment opportunities. Almost twenty years later I still carried that debt, more than a dozen years after grad school, considering it "good debt" since I read that it was *good* for your credit score if you maintained monthly payments for years, but Mamou encouraged me to wage war on it. I funneled every spare dollar into the Mohela site, selling most effects pedals, foregoing breakfast and as often as possible skipping lunch, subsisting throughout the day on free black coffee at work and water, doing so without a problem or much discomfort, benefiting from it financially and physically, the two united in this austerity plan.

I made my final loan repayment the same week the Notre Dame cathedral burned; a tornado complete with strobe lightning and hail rolled through Philadelphia at three in the morning, knocking down the sole large tree on our block across from our place; we toured the house with the porch and two huge trees out front a second time and our bid, submitted on Good Friday, was accepted; the long-awaited Mueller Report was released; and my father fell and was institutionalized. Everything resolving at once, the week ending on an Easter Sunday visit to my parents' place, oddly giddy that my father was in the hospital and wasn't home. Simultaneity of this sort Faulkner called "the passion week of the heart."

What would happen with my father? How would emerging Alzheimer's upset his long-established stability? Sudden trauma (car crash)? Something more gradual leading to institutionalization? Would careless online activity bankrupt the family? Would he somehow undermine my mother's late-life security? And at the same time questions of *if* or *when* we'd move from city to suburbs were answered, even if we'd always considered a move unlikely. Now we knew where and when we'd move, time and space coordinates secured. *Would I ever repay my graduate school loan?* was a lesser question also resolved.

I endured the simultaneity of these resolutions thanks in part to skipping breakfast and sometimes lunch. I overcame the vending machine by targeting protein, minimizing carbs, and avoiding sugar in all forms. I ascended stairs in bounds, healthier than I'd been in years, and so was able to deal when Mom called with a serious tone and news about what had happened to Dad.

I told her to wait a second as I walked to the bedroom and sat down in a chair by the window, expecting to hear that my father had died. But he had not died. He had fallen and hit his head, broke the towel rack in the bedroom bathroom, fell again in my former bedroom where he often sat at the computer or in bed watching TV. My mom found blood on a weight bench and drops on the white shag throw rug across the hardwood floor. He had a gash between his eyes, right where the third eye appears, he had cut himself there, where in the '70s a dermatologist had removed a mole that had always bothered him that had been in the same spot, eventual target for the wound that would move his story forward.

We now knew what would happen. My mother was telling me how it had happened. He hadn't died. He was still alive. It was a relief in a way to know what *would* happen, what *had* happened.

He fell, hit his head, wasn't making sense, disoriented, speech garbled, haggard, afraid, unwilling to go to the hospital.

Worried he'd grab the wheel or open the door if she got him in the car to go to the hospital, my mom called an ambulance. They strapped him against his will into a metal chair of some sort, hefted him from the second floor of the house he'd lived in since 1971 and haunted as a retiree since

1994, took him from the house, his car, tennis gear, tennis trophies, boxes of slides from vacations mostly to Greece in the past twenty years, Spanish language books notated with translations of words he'd looked up, everything left behind for good as he was carted to a hospital and examined, received stitches, they stabilized his knee which was weakened, and gave him something to mellow him out. He was seventy seven.

This is what it came down to, a major transitional node for my father and the family, the event that led to institutionalization.

What a word. *Institutionalization*: as long and as upright as a nursing home hallway. Five *i*'s: one for his youth, one for his adulthood, one for middle age, one for old age, and now this new identity as occupant of a memory care facility.

On Easter 2019 we visited him for the first time after the event. The hospital transformed in his mind into a dormitory as though he were back in college but also it was a hotel, like an all-inclusive Caribbean resort. He looked the same, his lower lip slack for some reason. He'd had a recent dental issue, a tooth fell out, his body falling apart from grains and sugar and chocolate and ice cream. He'd played doubles tennis but never walked or gardened although he lifted weights and exercised on the floor of his room, leg lifts, that sort of thing. He'd lost muscle definition in his legs a few years before the event, wasting away, the skin on his chest marked by scars from visits to the dermatologist who removed precancerous benign growths from decades lying out on the back patio, reading with shirt off and shorts hiked or just lying there, turning every twenty minutes, feeling the sun irradiate him, dry flaky skin improved by lotion and solar exposure. In summer, coming through the back door, sunglasses still on, white tennis hat low, shirt off, soft belly and love handles and toned chest browned, approaching black in the shade of the living room, a little sweaty, in search of a glass of water. He had an athletic mentality that simplified, did what was necessary and not much more, his keyword "methodical," a good mind for math, able to do complicated calculations in his head, visualizing it.

In winter it's like he didn't exist. He mobilized when I was young to shovel snow or sat on the orange shag-rug floor to watch a football game with me, his back to the couch so he could pet the collie beside him, but he wasn't in his element, needed to live in Florida, California, Arizona, wherever the sun more often shone than not. He wasn't spiritual but nonchalantly worshipped the sun and loved to sweat, best achieved via tennis, his primary social interaction on the court, his contact with other people mostly related to arranging matches.

Never smoked, never drank.

I drank more on December 28, 2019 before heading to the Garden than my father drank in his life in my presence. I'd gone through peaks and troughs with drinking, only beer really, sometimes getting a little carried away with it, sometimes cutting it out for weeks. I liked the effect, the styles, the taste, the satisfaction of it. By the end of 2019 I was drinking daily beer again after a party in mid-October we had on a Saturday to open our new house to friends to come see it and us. I bought enough beer if no one brought anything but friends brought their own and left it so afterwards I had at least fifty random craft bottles to savor after work as I made dinner and streamed to a portable wireless speaker studio albums by the band I had never heard (had stopped listening to them in college, surprised by the quality of their "recent" output, dozens of live and studio albums released in the past quarter century), kitchen windows open as I barbecued, dusk coming earlier each day, leaves in dying bloom, hoodie sweatshirt in service again, buzzed by it all, feeling good, eating well, Kali happily transforming into something half-human/half-tablet.

I tell her about when I was a kid, the handful of channels, antenna atop the house, the archaic experience of someone unfortunate enough to live before the internet. Way back when in the Dark Ages, I spent hours in front of the TV, drawing, organizing baseball cards, playing as I watched whatever shows were on, limited by what was on when, what must seem like inconceivable passivity as she switches between YouTube and apps installed for free, asking me to download another one, whining when I refuse because it costs $4.99, aware this will evolve to asking for cash (if cash still exists) to go to a movie (if theaters still exist) with friends in six or seven years, happy to pay for a silent, empty house where I can straighten everything disordered throughout the week.

A single person can make changes, can analyze and optimize, can tighten things up and give themselves some slack. But co-managing a house and family processes, it's almost impossible to optimize when two of the three family members are blurs, moving unnecessary objects around, having no time because their time is spent moving unnecessary objects around, unconsciously covering every surface with stuff (the word *stuff* is perfect, verb and noun).

As I wrote the word *stuff,* Mamou interrupted to show an ottoman she just unpacked in the form of a sheep she'd earned through a program at work in which colleagues assign points to one another to recognize and reward good behavior, helpfulness, inspiration, whatever. She had nine-thousand good-behavior points and the sheep ottoman cost nine-thousand points so she selected it from the catalog of redeemable rewards.

I said *good,* finally a piece of furniture in the house for me to fuck.

Which she didn't appreciate.

More clutter, more stuff, now in the form of a sheep on which to rest our feet.

I tell myself the upheaval will settle, Kali will settle, Mamou will settle, the way one of our cats had been so rambunctious as a kitten but now that he's older and can spend every third night out on the hunt, he's ideal, living his best cat life. There's hope for the future. But recently, this fall, since the housewarming party, daily beer, darkness arriving earlier each day, I've felt like a bulb of garlic overexposed to sunlight and starting to rot.* I've found it hard to maintain a positive outlook, to consider everything with general positive regard, worn down by the commute, not exercising, exposed to the same people every day on the train, frumpiness, bulbousness, stylishlessness, a situation or environment or surroundings I've tried to avoid all my adult life, expecting more for some reason from a suburban commuter train, even one that leaves the station a four-minute walk away from our house at 5:34, *an extreme hour* I once would've thought, something only doable if I get to sleep by nine, waking at 4:45, dressing, running water through hair, downing iced coffee, sitting for five minutes with my laptop to respond to easy work emails that push things forward so by the time I arrive at the office at 6:30 I might have responses, and then reading on the train.

With morning sun the train was glorious at first, gorgeous, the earliest summer light on unfamiliar stations before we reached the city. But now dark windows reflect passengers sitting in silence in the quiet ride car. And then the two people I most often talked with at work both left *on the same day* in early November, one of them the guy who'd changed my life after a quick conversation about nutrition, the other not wanting in general to oversee monthly clinical journals and manage a pair of co-dependent assistant managers who everyone thought were romantically involved, the guy an older married right-winger from Delaware who expresses himself by changing his desktop

---

* Is that an effective simile? Maybe so, maybe not.

image to comment on the news. For example during the Brett Kavanaugh hearings he had an image of Lindsay Graham shouting down the woman who accused Kavanaugh of sexual assault. I posted a photo of his Lindsay Graham desktop image to Instagram with some fiery text, deleted it, fumed about it, waited for it to change and then after he'd left it up for days I told him it was inappropriate and divisive in an office setting, particularly since it was in the context of sexual assault and our office is mostly women.

He said *oh I'm sorry I offended you*, suggesting I was a snowflake.

I said you didn't offend me, I can't be offended.

I said several times it was *inappropriate and divisive* in an office setting and he should change it to an Eagles logo or something neutral like that.

He said *you gonna report me to HR?*

I said I'm talking to you about it instead of talking to HR.

He said *OK I'll change it, I'll change it*, but then he didn't change it, and then as I ran out of the office because Kali had another incident at school I saw him and his codependent manager friend vaping outside the building.

An accretion of annoyance, frustration, a buildup of bullshit that makes it hard to see the good, move toward the good, confronted by all that is not good, not necessarily evil, but just not all that joyous, friendly, creative, kind. All those simplicities on the positive side of the spectrum.

His desktop. *Man, fuck his desktop.*

So many times while he was out vaping with his codependent manager friend I wanted to affix a desktop-denouncing Post-it to the "party-size" Cheez-It box he and his friend snacked on all day.

His desktop usually shows some variety of American flag, a macho dystopian version that seems degraded or in tatters or fragmented or darkened and run through by a blue line, his favorite, his default, his son a cop now after a few years in the service, stationed in Hawaii.

The blueline flag suggests a thin blue line between order and chaos but in recent years seems like the fascist flag or at least you see it on pickups and in front of houses explicitly supporting Trump even without an election imminent. The flag supports law and order even if most who fly it claim to be libertarians, seeing no conflict between their love of law and order and the lawlessness of their president and his disrespect for the Constitution, the true king of the country since inception.

Their allegiance is based on a sort of faith that has nothing to do with God or religion or spirituality but what they believe is good: the police, small government, so-called patriotism, the military, in some cases supremacy of the white Christian male. Those who oppose everything they believe is good are bad. Separation of everything into good and bad is right and natural. Guns are good, people are bad. Abortion is bad, adoption is good. Taxes should be low, the government shouldn't help the poor, money should go to the military and border control.

Only because the guy in the office next to mine arranged his computer so the monitors are visible from the doorway do I see his political expressions and fume about them as I refill my coffee cup and water bottle or visit the bathroom. Whenever I walk by, I have to tell myself he's not the embodiment of the enemy ideology, he's a victim of Fox News exposure and poor education, his moral compass skewed by processed carbohydrates and crap beer and the indignity of having a prior editorial office job outsourced to India, an insult to his ego and sense of American exceptionalism.

He's maybe ten years older than I am, belly growing out faster than legs and face, steel-framed glasses and gray little cop mustache, had a stent installed a year ago. Only because he occupies the office next to mine do I concern myself with him. If he sat *anywhere else* I wouldn't worry about him, would talk sports whenever an encounter were unavoidable, and would chat with whoever occupied the office next to mine the way I used to chat with him before the 2016 election, often about the local professional basketball team's intentional super-subpar performance. He was against it, swayed by the worst sportswriters and talk radio personalities.

Positions on "The Process" anticipated the election since younger fans understood what's required to contend for a championship in contemporary professional basketball, how losing could yield winning after drafting a generational talent who could improve a team for a decade, younger fans understood what it took to avoid perpetual first-round playoff-exit limbo but older fans for the most part and those swayed by the worst sportswriters believed the point was to put the best team on the floor every year and win as many games as possible. Intentionally losing now to win later seemed against the social contract, breaking the rules they love to support except when the police or the military or their politicians bend or break the law.

Now a few years later the local professional basketball team regularly competes for a championship thanks to exceptional young players but the lesson of flexibility and complexity and contrarian thinking doesn't sink in. It's still right and wrong, law and order, black and white separated by a thin blue line.

I forget about him and his friend as soon as I leave work, rarely mention them at dinner, but once I return to the office, my spirit sinks. Practicing contempt more than compassion, recognizing something wrong and instead of feeling for them, I separate myself from them, presenting the appearance of not giving a shit about their presence, aware this too shall pass, temporary proximity the only reason I interact with them. I won't always see his desktop every time I leave my office. There's got to be something more than this, somewhere I could work with colleagues I respect, such colleagues have worked here for a few years before they leave, same as everyone leaves other than a handful of lifers.

Somehow I became a lifer, same way my father worked at one company for thirty years, never moving for more money and acclimating to a similar workflow with different acronyms, having to learn procedures again, start from scratch with no institutional knowledge, rebuild a good reputation, not to mention losing perks of seniority like extra accrued vacation days, in my case also possibly losing casual dress, a work-from-home option once a week, summer hours, most likely definitely losing general autonomy, possibly also losing the ability to listen to music all day through sweet headphones, familiarity with the systems and casual mastery of the processes, also a sense that the company intends to exist in the world and in the lives of its employees as a force for good (more than it wants to maximize profits and control souls), so it doesn't make sense to move for the sake of a little more money. I'd just have to work that much harder to achieve what I have now, always comparing the new situation with the old one, wondering if the change improved my life, plus working in the same office now for thirteen years I get to practice my favorite skill developed over the years: endure, persist, stay on the bus, see storms gather, crash, pass, and clear, stick with it, not give up, work through it, take a break and return with fresh eyes, remove emotion and get above it, see the topography for what it is, rippling hills overcome with time and effort, not mountains or anything resembling mountains.

But removal of emotion can become a habit, lead to cycles of boredom, regret, neglect, disengagement, degraded perception of a world reduced to train and office and walks to and from both, everything reduced to something too small and regular and controlled even if I correspond every day with authors and editors all over the world, working globally but only on a textual basis, this idealized realm of correspondence where I am confident in my abilities and presentation of professional editorial affability.

I work on illustrated books by radiologists, pathologists, dermatologists, cardiologists, oncologists, gastroenterologists, ophthalmologists, and surgeons of all sorts. It's considered editorial but I'm more of a project manager, not making many old-fashioned editorial decisions or copyediting except when integrating author/editor corrections. Whatever I do during the weekdays, earning money, securing stability and good health insurance for the family, being a good husband and dad, being in a word *responsible*, waking up too early, reading on train, walking to office before dawn, working, walking around at lunch, working, walking to train, reading on train, cooking dinner, watching television with Mamou and Kali, getting to bed early to wake up early, it's all been wearing me down more than when I used to walk to work, waking up early to write or run or read, morning time reserved for personal production and progress, time carved out super-early now transmuted into the commute.

Before the move I had been writing about a weekend afternoon in mid-November 2018, waiting for Mamou in the car at the South Philadelphia Walmart with Kali in the back maybe having to pee, the car key turned ahead to let the radio stream the Grateful Dead satellite station as I looked at my phone, increasingly agitated as ten minutes became twenty minutes and then thirty minutes. I felt like I could write about it forever but then the move from the city interceded, daily excitement and practice of working on it stalled, and by the time we unpacked in the new house and I tried to work on it again I'd lost the edge, the wave had passed, and what had seemed limitless, a short novel for sure, I whittled to a story.

Since then, until now, the first weeks of 2020, thumbing this out on my phone while taking the early train, I've been feeling like I can't even commit to keeping at it and doing it for its own sake, the standard palliative justifications, all the talk about books and writing, immersion in related news and activities as though it were some religious sect, the problem being that I'd thought of it as a religious practice, which has nothing to do with the practices of publishing, confronting the challenges of no longer being all that young, not being representative of a place or a type of person, and writing in a style not of interest to those interested in experimental prose but also not accessible or formulaic enough to please readers accustomed to conventional narrative. On top of that, the stories I wrote weren't stories so much as static opportunities for digressive associative rumination.

The Process

This is how I live my life. Why weekdays are spent defer-
ring gratification at work. To sit, to wait—trapped in the
car for half an hour on a Saturday as wife shops in a big
box store. Unable to make a decision, distracted by every
sparkly item, has she forgotten her five-year-old daughter
sits behind me in the back seat, overdue for an opportunity
to ward off a pee emergency?

Kali peed herself frequently and excessively at school.
She crouched and peed through her pants all over her
kindergarten floor, six times in a single day. I left work
and took her to the doctor who ruled out diabetes, said she
didn't have an infection, it was probably caused by stress.
Another time, in the school bathroom, she peed on the
floor through her pants and then threw her backup pair
into the toilet. Given another pair she threw those in too.

Teachers can't use force against our child, not even if we
issue written permission, a restraining order of sorts. They
can only deploy voice commands she might not even register. Humming ventilator unit, reflection of sun on window
across street, every sensory input competes for attention,
or so I'm told. She should attend school in the woods, on
a beach, not in a classroom where she can't control her im-
pulses.

She could pee her car seat any minute. It's a ticking
timebomb back there. And in the front seat what's the

point? Why do I make an effort? Why did I marry someone willing to spend half an hour in a box store, someone who *prefers* big box stores because her family didn't have much money when growing up in a small midwestern town?

More than a decade ago after graduate school in a small midwestern town I should have returned to Brooklyn or gone to Los Angeles, San Francisco, Portland, Chicago. I could have moved anywhere. Quetzaltenango, Ouagadougou, Ulaanbaatar. Instead I returned close to where I grew up, near where elderly parents still live. I moved to a city with potential, with upside, with ground to cover between ideal version and current reality. I could have gone anywhere but instead selected the least expensive large city in the Northeast, and I got what I paid for, sitting in this parking lot, scanning preset satellite radio stations, hoping our daughter doesn't pee.

Mamou has an hour and a half commute each way to a stressful job that pays more than twice what mine does, which severely undercuts all complaint, I realize. But still the burden falls on me to keep it together, to get Kali ready and take her to school, bring her home, help with homework, make dinner with real food. Everything edible in that box store is filled with noxious industrial seed oils, sugar in all its forms, processed carbohydrates designed to make humanity reliant on medications to treat the consequences of the poison they buy in these stores.

Jesus CHRIST how long has it been? We could have walked to the pier, Kali could have crouched behind a shrub if necessary, if I knew we had *more than half an hour*, even if it's windy and raw, glary, the sky diffused with smoke from fires on the other side of the country, or so I just read on my phone.

This parking lot and surrounding box stores imposed over the natural world, the river beds—there could be lovely parks down here but when they built this complex the river stank. Now that it's cleaner and doesn't smell, it all seems like wasted space.

I just want to go to New York by myself one weekend and see old friends and drink too much and take the last train back or crash on a couch and return in the morning. I want to do that twice a year. I should insist on it but Kali is too much for Mamou to handle alone. She goes to conferences for work, three nights away, and I handle the child no problem, but even one night solo seems like too much for her. She's stressed at work, up for a promotion, frazzled as external candidates interview for the job she's been doing on an interim basis. They've brought back an older boring white woman for multiple interviews. The company is methodical, slow to make decisions, possibly sending a message to everyone that they're deeply considering the position when they have the perfect candidate available internally. Mamou self-identifies as a superhero at work, needing the structure to motivate her and succeed. Half-Thai, Ivy-educated, and a well-fit woman, she's unlike the doughy white men in upper management, which may help or hurt her. But the decision process and this interim era is going on too long. It's affecting her and spilling over at home.

We're also waiting for our behavioral health rehabilitation service (BHRS) to send a functional behavioral assessment (FBA) to Community Behavioral Health (CBH) so CBH can decide to assign a therapeutic support specialist (TSS) to work with Kali throughout the day and make it easier for her teachers and other students. This has been the most difficult part of parenthood, navigating mental health services to receive city/state-provided certified help in the classroom. It began a year ago with an application for Medical Assistance (MA), following-up to ensure that the application went through, sending forms that hadn't been processed, following-up until we received MA, making an appointment with the BRHS known by its own four-letter acronym (NETC) that assigns a TSS after CBH approves an application based on multiple evaluations with redundant questions, never mind the seventy-page PDF for our daughter's Individualized Education Program (IEP) documenting everything. After each evaluation with NETC I followed-up to ensure they scheduled the next redundant evaluation and submitted half vacation days and left work to respond in person to redundant questions as Kali, pulled from school for each evaluation, burned through data on my phone. The process doesn't seem about helping parents get kids help. It's labyrinthine and slow to the point of immorality, braindead by design, or so I suspect.

We're waiting on CBH's final assessment before they assign a one-to-one, a wraparound, a TSS, whatever they call the human being dedicated to keeping Kali safe and compliant in school. Mamou waits on a decision about her job.

I recently found out that my boss of many years will no longer be my boss and instead I will have a new boss based in New York. After years of stability at work I don't know what will happen. My position could be eliminated. All submissions sent out this year have received encouraging rejections or I'm still waiting on responses nearly a year after submission. All savings goes to aggressively repaying grad school loans, which seems like unraveling my MFA, wiping the slate. I should delete all unpublishable novels and stories, damn it all and move on, but to where and to what? Without decades-established, dedicated creative processes for the most part yielding meager results, who am I? What am I? Someone who sits in the car and waits for his wife et cetera.

Maybe she's been arrested or had a heart attack or a psychotic break? Acting as interim head of her department as she interviews for the position. Knowing they're interviewing other candidates. I can't imagine dealing as well as she has, even if the stress, the commute, and coming home to her hyperactive daughter and a husband who's not always a ray of sunshine has been making her behave a little oddly lately.

In the eight years we've been together I've worried that if something happened to me she would become a full-blown hoarder. Nascent symptoms involve cardboard boxes in which she's placed bags incompletely filled with inconsequential anti-necessities, including another bag in which for example there's a box incompletely filled with colored paperclips for some forgotten craft project. She relaxes by working on her organizer, a functional future-event stabilizing craft project, an artistic meditative process by which she stabilizes the sense that there's so much to accomplish, so many demands on her, so little time, and endless possibilities, each branching into infinite possibilities. To limit the sense of infinite possibilities, to optimize an order of operations, she works on her planner, which requires a trip to the big box store, which she says dedicates an aisle to good cheap planner-related accessories—stickers, glitter, Post-its, everything needed to artfully organize to-do lists, manage calendars, and itinerate daily existence, which runs counter to what I do.

At work, I list what needs to be done, with the most pressing tasks at the top. I move through the list based on energy level and concentration capacity. I do, and then I write down what I did. I maintain an individual log for each project, as well as a comprehensive log, a spreadsheet with seven columns and a row for each of the fifty-plus projects assigned to me. With everything recorded, I have no need to remember.

For everything outside of work I maintain a separate spreadsheet too. Each day has its own row, logging in seven or so columns everything I ate, drank, wrote and read, the time I went to sleep and when I woke up, any exercise and how many steps I took, money spent and on what, the weather and general vibe, my weight if I can remember to step on the scale, and then an open cell for quick memory triggers for later review, notes about something Kali said or did, spats with Mamou or good times, things to remember, whatever I'm liable to forget. My grandfather thirty years ago and my father more recently developed memory issues related to dementia, so I'm compelled by the prospect of approaching forgetfulness, distortion, conflation if not yet confabulation. Although there's something confabulatory by definition about organizing the past this way. Writing on paper in black ink, typing it to review and edit to transfer an experience to a reader. To untangle the impressions of a series of moments, to present them as orderly and unified in language. As artificial and artful an activity as anything Mamou does with her planner.

Her activity looks to the future. It's private (unless she posts selections to Instagram), functional, and way more crafty and colorful with stickers and sparkles than whatever I do with pen and ink. But the instinct is similar. Ordering events unfolding in the past or future.

She's been dealing relatively well with future work-related uncertainty but still, on two occasions in recent weeks, she's exhibited disconcerting, irrational behavior. Now, sitting in the car, I'm concerned that a third instance in the big box store accounts for her delayed return.

A few weeks ago, nearly two months before Christmas, I asked Mamou to forward from her phone images my mother had seen and liked so I could print and frame them for a present. It wasn't an urgent request but, because she was sending her brother photographs at that moment, this *incursion* of a request, no matter how simple, seemed unfathomable. She flipped as though I had asked her to perform some intricate, intolerable, incomprehensibly arduous task. Also on the photographs printed at CVS a block from our house there were extraneous borders. How did I manage to pick them up but not review them before paying? What sort of half-wit pays for photos before looking at them to see if they're OK?

She said aggressive, condescending things, spurred by my request to send two images from her phone, not now, not this minute, for a Christmas present for my mother.

Mamou aggressively condescended. I left the room instead of retaliating.

But then I returned because I didn't want her alone with our child in such a state, totally irrational, aggressive, and just plain mean.

I screamed at her in a way that made Kali jump on her mother to protect her, telling her mother to stop what she was saying, settle down, shut her mouth.

This instinct our daughter has to settle the fight. Instead of cowering and crying, her eyes alight as she diagnoses the situation in an instant and shushes the one in the wrong, the parent freaking out, unleashing tension on the other, before everything settles as though none of it ever happened. This instance of one parent freaking out on the other occurred I think because Mamou had attended a strenuous weight-lifting exercise class earlier in the day and was amped on whatever hormones were excreted.

She once said she had too much testosterone, which accounts for having the body of an Olympic athlete. A rower in college, she's been training for an indoor competition, excited to discover a subculture devoted to the ergonomic rowing machine. She's been weight training to improve her performance. All of which seems better than watching TV and eating chips but I've noticed some adverse effects like aggression, obsessive-compulsion, condescension.

Last weekend she lifted weights in the living room, thirty sets of twelve-repetition squats and jerks with ten-pound barbells, and then later in the day she committed to untangling the cord for the headphones Kali wears when watching her tablet. She untangled the cord for hours, sitting on the couch in her cluttered nook. Whenever I tried to politely ask what she was doing she blamed and demeaned everyone for letting the cord get so tangled.

I watched three quarters of the hometown professional football team's first game of the season against a good team. The previous season the team had won the league's last game on February 4, 2018, the first time the team had won it all. The victory sent the city and surrounding region into absolute ecstasy, fulfilling everyone's lifelong dream of seeing the team win the big game. But on the night of the unknotting, the local professional football team was getting crushed. It wasn't worth watching and absorbing the negativity. On the night of the unknotting I turned the game off before it was over, something I rarely do.

Whenever I passed Mamou's nook that night where she sat on a love seat alone, cross-legged, deeply engaged in this free analogue activity of untangling the headphone cord, I made a happy little comment like you're so obviously procrastinating right now.

Hours later, after I put Kali to bed, I asked Mamou, in the kindest possible tone, if I should call an ambulance to convey her to the nearest psychiatric ward.

She laughed at this, aware that untangling the cord had become a puzzle she needed to solve, something that couldn't be left unfinished, even if so much of what she starts remains incomplete. Unloading the dishwasher, she only puts away twelve items because she has a number-twelve fixation. She counts not to ten but to twelve, sets timers for twelve minutes but then stops what she's doing after twelve minutes even if it's a fifteen-minute task.

The next morning she left before seven to catch a bus to a train to a car she parks at a distant station to drive to her office. I found the headphones on the couch in her nook. After all those hours of work the cord was still tangled.

I failed to make progress for a minute, so I pulled the cord ends to lengthen it as long as possible, taped the most-knotted parts into a gray transparent clump, and taped the section of the cord liable to knot later on. It wasn't pretty but it was functional, somewhat neater, and fine for Kali to use at her after-school program, or in the back of a black Subaru Forester.

Behind me in her car seat, on her tablet with head-phones on, Kali asks if Mamou is coming back soon?

Now that she's older she's begun to repeat what we say. I need to control my response, so I don't say yeah where is she, huh? Your freaking mother! Totally inconsiderate. Buying crap at the most vile store in America while we sit in the parking lot and rot. What the fuck, baby?

Instead I reduce its expression to a groan as a Lexus sedan pulls in front of us. A young mother, maybe Argentine or Lebanese, and her three children are driven by an older man, possibly their father, in dark jeans and Patagonia jacket. He dyes his hair so it's as dark as that of his three boys. Her hair is equally dark, dressed in jeans and a black puffy coat. Her face is beautiful, her skin golden, radiant, pure, and she handles the three boys with grace as the father retrieves a shopping cart and releases a flier from inside it, just lifts it and lets the wind carry it toward the river. They make their way, the five of them, toward the store with their cart.

It never occurred to me to take Kali and venture inside with Mamou. I need to protect myself from the high ceiling lined with uncovered fluorescent bulbs that cause slight yet perceptible neurological damage. They're all flashing on and off a million times a second, conspiring with the dyes in the towels, the unnatural fresh scents, and the general consumerist glare to reduce my desire to wanting nothing to do with it. And then the human beings encountered therein of course induce contempt and compassion in eternal round, mothers screaming at their kids, borderline beating them in public. At a glance they turn your stomach and break your heart, alleviate in comparison your burdens and hardships. The diabetic bruises around their ankles, the discomfort and suffering, making such an effort to shop for exactly the products that contribute to their conditions. Yet there's no way you can intercede and knock the mega-size plastic barrel of gummy worms from their hands.

No matter how bad it's becoming in the car, it would be several times worse in the store. There's no way we're going in there. We're waiting this out. I imagine Saturday afternoon becoming Saturday evening, Sunday morning, Sunday afternoon, all without leaving the car. We'll order delivery to our parking space, hold excretions, Kali's tablet recharging thanks to the intensity of her attention. Or I suppose it would be worse if we were irrational aspirants who couldn't afford anything in the store yet spent weekends pretending to shop, comparing prices, miming putting items in empty shopping carts we pushed through the store.

And just like that Mamou returns.

It had only been about half an hour lost forever from our lives.

The ordeal is over! Hurrah! Let's roll!

She settles into the passenger seat. "You need to pee, honey? Should we hit the potty before we go?"

"I don't have to pee," says a cute little voice behind us.

I look in the rear-view mirror. Kali looks at tablet. "I'll pee tomollow," she says, the Rs not yet settled in place, their slots first occupied like baby teeth by cute yet incorrect Ls.

If she were lost I would report her identifying characteristics as a single small mole about an inch from her armpit toward her chest and a tendency to say "tomorrow" with

Ls instead of Rs, maybe something she shares with her maternal grandmother from Thailand.

Before I start the car, Mamou shows me the inexpensive crafting supplies she secured to assist her organizing work, something I may have criticized in my bachelorhood but now see as an idea like all others that breaches the surface and recedes, half-completed, before some new idea catches her interest. She's acquired fingertip-sized stickers in the form of stars, hearts, rainbows, gold-plated or encrusted with glitter, also miniature Post-it notes, bright strips for color-coding systems, prioritizing, prettifying future progress through upcoming days.

"Cherry Hill Mall?" I say and turn the key from its slightly turned position that let us listen to the radio as we waited.

I turn it again and give it some gas like it's the old Volvo I used to have that often had trouble starting.

I pull the key out and try it again.

The radio works. The lights on the dashboard are lit. But the engine won't activate, engage, combust, simply fucking start.

I hadn't even really been listening to the radio, just had music on out of habit, and now we're stuck, our plans, as meager as they were, dashed. The distance between location and destination infinitely increased.

I'm calm, maybe because I haven't eaten yet or because I've been less reactive since I stopped eating sugar and carbs five months earlier, or maybe I'm simply focused on figuring out what we need to do to start the engine again and leave this parking lot.

We scramble in the glove compartment for the insurance company's roadside assistance number. I just called them a few weeks ago about some damage to the front end of the car. They were clear, helpful, and kind, soothing without sounding false. The guy who helped me had a light Southern accent, suggestive of a different climate and culture, a way of life where everyone intuits that your battery has died and brings their car around to offer a jump, or they'll have their own automotive IEDs, those portable rechargers, and send you on your way.

It turns out we don't have roadside assistance through our insurance company for this car, something Mamou believes is false and states harshly as I'm on the phone. We then call Subaru's roadside assistance, who we must have called the last time Kali had switched on the light above the backseat and it was left on all night and drained our battery. A guy came out within an hour, started the car in seconds, and told me to run it for half an hour, which I did as I read a friend's novel about mass shootings in America, parked along a city street on a Saturday afternoon, running the engine, wondering what hot topics I could write about instead of whatever I write about. The battery must have been degraded by that experience. Maybe that's why it drained again from listening to the radio for half an hour?

It doesn't matter how it happened. It's happened and now we have to deal.

Mamou provides our approximate coordinates in the lot. I'm sure we'll be easy to find among the similarly shaped, sized, and colored vehicles, our aerodynamic bulbous transportation beetle still with a year-old dent on the right rear bumper, particularizing it, giving it character.

The car parked behind ours on a narrow side street had been hit in such a way that the complete front bumper unit had fallen off. We had been hit too but only suffered a grapefruit-sized dimple on the right rear bumper. I watched a video called "how to fix a dent with a plunger and a blowtorch" but I didn't have a blowtorch handy and didn't run out to get one. A year passed. The dent bothered me but not enough to get it fixed. Then on a weekend morning a month ago we again noticed that someone had hit us. This time we'd been sideswiped. There were scrapes along the wheel and hubcap and the front end had detached an inch or two. A thousand dollar deductible claimed a week later it looked good as new except we didn't get the back dent fixed. It wasn't part of the insurance claim, so they returned it with dent intact, which was fine since the dent differentiated our black Forester from three others on the block.

On the list of everything we need to take care of sooner or later, the dent is more of a symbolic parallel for this time in our lives than it is a priority. It won't always be this way. It will get better, we say to ourselves. Whenever I say this I envision the teenage version of our hyperactive, curious, willful child smiling at our naivety. In ten years, we'll be even more worn down, unable to follow an adolescent jettisoned at warp speed into inevitable independence.

Roadside assistance says they'll arrive in an hour. Mamou leaves to upgrade her phone at an AT&T store in the complex and find something to eat. I sit in the car, now with more time to read my phone, ask Kali if she needs to pee every few minutes, and otherwise wait.

It's my fault. I ran the battery down listening to the radio. But she also took forever in the big box store. I can't believe we'll spend more time here.

As we wait for roadside assistance I read about the local professional basketball team's most recent game. It was among the first after a trade considered the end of The Process, the team's attempt to become a perennial championship contender by losing games, developing young undrafted players, and maximizing salary space and chances of drafting at least one generational talent who alone can change a team's fortunes. I intensely supported suffering through an intentional period of losing if it meant a chance at a dynasty in time. There was something revelatory and artful about emphasizing Process over Results in the context of professional sports, something counterintuitive and beautiful.

I read all the articles about the local professional basketball team's most recent game. The newly acquired star hit a buzzer beater in overtime to secure the win as the crowd went wild. The team was winning more games now but something seemed lost, like when your favorite unknown band starts playing arenas.

After we were married, my wife's very gay friend from college, the illegitimate son of a Swedish model and a Moroccan prince, told me something I've since accepted as absolutely true: the secret to getting along with your new wife, he said, is to respond to everything she says with "that's a good idea!" Nod your head with enthusiasm and never dismiss or second guess her, which will unleash condescension and hurt. But if you engage the idea with *instantaneous positive reinforcement*, the idea will go away before the next one emerges in half an hour.

Every night in her early teens Mamou had to use a fine-toothed plastic comb to remove excessive plaque from her older sister's scalp. What looked like scales, scabs, often bloody, kept coming non-stop thanks to serious psoriatic arthritis. This older sister, now an activist for disabled rights, Mamou's role model growing up, so confident, lithe, and coordinated, was wrenched by the overproduction of skin cells, her fingers gnarled in claw-like shapes. She was in part my wife's responsibility as a child but also the young Mamou often thought why wasn't she the one who got sick? Why did her sister get all the attention? Why was her childhood marked by having to care for someone so revered and close, but also couldn't this happen to her any second? Every aching shinbone from a growth spurt, could it be the start of something that would mark her for the rest of her life? And who would take care of her older sister, her younger siblings still too young for this, and anyway it was her responsibility to help her sister and protect her younger brother and sister from removing over-replicated skin so tomorrow's surge of new skin had a place to go without excessive pile-up.

We were engaged by the time I met her family. Like crazy people in love we purchased a home six months after meeting, caught in the flow of mutual will to such a degree it seemed fated. It wasn't prudent but it wasn't so much a reasonable decision as it was an action. We could do it and so we did it. It wasn't like we discussed next steps. There was an unspoken assumption she could buy me out if necessary or we'd sell if it wasn't working but a year exactly after meeting we were married and a year after that she was pregnant with the child now in the backseat, all set to wait to pee until tomorrow, forty-one years and two days younger than her father, thirty-six years younger than her mother.

We were older when we met and so were able to move forward in haste. We had been through the rise and fall of relationships so many times we knew when it felt right. The minor annoyances of another human being's humanhood might be manageable this time when they hadn't been in the past, in part because certain key facts were not aired until after marriage and pregnancy. Only after our DNA had intertwined and the cells inside her had replicated to the point of viability did I learn certain biographical facts that may have been too much for me when considered with everything else I had come to know about her and her family. More so, beyond facts later revealed, there was the complication of her Thai mother, but also her right-wing father, a family in general so particular and isolated that it has charisma, its eccentricity and disorder so much rangier than the family I grew up in as an only child like our daughter now, our little power trio extended into a quintet with feline support players.

I didn't consider her family a factor until it was too late. I was informed by Mamou's brother's wife that, as the new one, there would be a hazing period, an era of criticism that, I suppose because I was removed from them by the states of Pennsylvania and Ohio for all but a few days a year, I overcame with apathy and counter-criticism. They may have imagined someone else for the child they put through a top-tier Ivy, the most traditionally successful and "smartest" of their four children, the one who did best on standardized tests, ran the fastest, had the most robust physical form and a rambunctious, restless, irrepressible spirit and sparkle in the eye, a real dynamo, who's chosen for her mate not some financial powerhouse in Manhattan or corporate lawyer who used to row at an Ivy too but a writer of uneventful autobiographical essayistic stories, someone with zero interest in Corvettes or cars in general, someone who takes pleasure in sitting alone with a long old novel but when asked what he's learned from all the books on his shelves, instead of delivering a quotation from Tolstoy or Chekhov or an original epigrammatic reduction he concocts on the spot about the search for meaning in a mysterious world, about artfully ordering the chaos of experience, he sincerely talks about how each book is a souvenir, like a plastic figurine of a famous attraction that evokes a few days' stay in a limitless city, and also a souvenir that can be experienced again differently on demand. It's not like they're manuals delivering step-by-step instructions or histories filled with dates and occasions or even riveting tales that can be retold around a dinner table, ideally at a diner since we've learned that her father loves driving to diners where he can chat up the waitresses and dislikes restaurants to which we can walk that have vegan options and young tattooed servers et cetera. But for a former Air Force engineer the notion of a wall of experiences, of obliquely functional expressions of life in individuated language, ideally engaging, insightful, perception-enhancing, forward-flowing, often gorgeous, maybe he'd understand in terms of a Corvette representing something more than a mode of transportation?

I sometimes, particularly early on, dreamed of an ideal in-law family, the sort I would drive entire days to see with pleasure, joking that I felt like I was finally home whenever I visited them, but once we had Kali I no longer cared. All the elements had combined to the point of inevitability, without one of which we wouldn't have married and made this kid, the point of all of it now in the backseat on her tablet, this kid who doesn't need to pee, and if all goes well will in about half an hour be seated in a booth at a high-end chain restaurant appended to an gargantuan New Jersey mall, happily eating grilled chicken, green beans, and mashed potatoes, the finest kids meal in the area by far, worth more than the extra three dollars over competitor kids meals.

Parenthood opens us to new experiences as much as it closes possibilities. I wake up at hours once considered cruel just to sit quietly, drink coffee, and read. Like an old friend, I make an effort to stay in touch with solitude. We meet under the cover of darkness, or in the summer, well before six, the sun rising as I run through empty city streets, essentially alone for half an hour or forty-five minutes. Soon, in just a few years, she'll assert her independence. She'll go on outings with her mother, will have activities I don't need to supervise or attend, will go for walks alone, or will stay over at a friend's house. In only a few years. Already she's almost able to make the successful journey to the movie theater about ten blocks away if handed a $20 bill.

We used to joke about how far she'd get if given twenty dollars and told where the movie theater was, how far she'd get before a stranger called the police or she got lost and cried, unable to give the coordinates of her house, or she got hit by a car crossing a street. Now she might be able to make it there but I can't imagine she'd manage to pay and find the room showing the movie she wanted to see in the multiplex after buying her popcorn, finding a seat, going to the bathroom if necessary, making her way all the way home when the movie lets out. It's terrifying to think of, the impossibility of walking a few blocks and seeing a movie and walking home, something she'll maybe do with friends in five years when she's ten?

My father, approaching eighty, won't walk around the block, let alone to the park and around its clearly defined paved paths, or of course the gravel paths in the woods beyond the park, the best part about where they live, this string of parks, four miles of lightly maintained woods, playing fields, ponds, ideal for long daily constitutionals. But my father won't even walk how he did when taking our old collie around the block in the late '70s at night under clear cold skies, pointing out Orion's belt like esoteric knowledge.

I was probably Kali's age when I first recognized Orion. Now she opens an app and all the constellations and planets come to life as she holds the phone to the sky, almost too much detail, most stars not making their way through the light pollution. I would have loved something like that when I was a kid with my father and the family dog, dead now almost forty years. I would have loved to know the names of the shapes I saw, the triangle, the one like a question mark.

At the end of *The Trial* (*Der Process* in Kafka's original German) when K. seeks admission to The Law, a guard with a huge Tartan beard impedes his progress and warns him that this entrance is only the first of many beyond it, each guarded by more fearsome guards. Even if he makes it past this first guard, there's no way he'll make it past the next one, or the next or the next or the next, each more fear-some than the last. After a lifetime waiting at the door with the guard, with his last breath, K. asks why no one else has ever come to this entrance seeking admission to the Law? The guard says because this door was only meant for you—and now I'm going to close it. Whereupon K. is van-quished to the ice mountains, lost forever, which is a refer-ence to the end of Kafka's "The Bucket Rider," another story of a solitary human seeking something (in the case of the story, coal). In both stories, the seeker is rejected in the end. But for us, at the end of *this* story, it'll feel like we've been granted a temporary exception.

Mamou returns from an unsuccessful trip to the AT&T store (long disgruntled lines, unhelpful employees) and a satisfying trip to McDonald's. She's brought chicken nuggets for Kali and the car smells like fast food so I leave them inside the car and expose myself to the smoke-diffused glare of the comparatively wide open sky of the big box store parking lot. It's like a lake of pavement, delineated into spaces, with raised walkways and streetlights. The sky seems rubbed out, blurred, too bright. The movement of cars and people below on the level of the parking lot seems insignificant, ant-like, reduced, desperate. I shade my eyes as I scan the parking lot for a stray roadside assistance ve-hicle coming for us. I wish we had a flag to fly or a flare gun. At most I could call and tell roadside assistance to look for a tall, middle-aged white guy repeatedly tossing a red, white, and blue, kid-size basketball overhead.

A busted old station wagon stops behind where we're parked. The windows are down, two kids in back, a woman in front. A man gets out of the idling car. He seems a little older than me, leathery and worn, his few remaining teeth exaggeratedly crooked. He wears soiled khakis and an oversized half-opened button-down short-sleeve shirt with flared collars.

He points at the dent. "Five minutes, I fix, wait here."

He returns to his car and moves it so it's not in the middle of the lane but as close as possible to two parked cars. He reemerges with a blowtorch and a hammer.

"Only five minutes, no more dent, you don't like it you no pay."

"Please don't blowtorch our car," I say, worried it will somehow explode.

"I fix it, no more."

"How much?"

"Forty."

"I don't have cash on me."

"Get it," he says, nodding toward the looming box store.

I tell him to wait a second. I explain the situation and ask Mamou in the passenger seat if she has forty bucks. She checks her wallet. "Go for it," she says, handing me two twenties.

The guy is already on his back, blowtorch in hand, heating and hammering the inside of the bumper, pushing the dented plastic out. Two minutes later he's spraying an epoxy on the bumper and wiping it clean.

"Wow," I say, "you did it."

He really did do it. It's not perfect, there are still some indentations, dimples, but it's comparatively fixed. I give him the money, laughing about how easy that was, but I'm skeptical too, thinking that as soon as he drives away it will pop back out.

"It'll stay like that?"

"It stay or I fix free." He says he's always driving around the lot.

I wonder if he drives around and dents cars, although it's unnecessary considering tight streets lined with cars, the number of bars, the moments of distraction.

I'm giddy, as though everything with our daughter, wife's work, my inability to find time for my so-called pre-ferred activities, all now is fixed, heated up, pushed out.

The roadside assistance guy is the same guy who came out last time. He has incredible eyes, light blue and large, dark lashes. He's otherwise a burly dude in a jump suit and wields the same portable battery-jumping device. I tell him about what just happened with the dent. He says there's gypsies all over these lots. They fix your dent fast but nowhere close to a pro job. I say I guess I'm easy to please.

The car turns over and he says to keep it running for half an hour, so we drive to an enormous mall across the Delaware River in New Jersey, eat at Seasons 52 (flatbread and salads and mini-indulgences all around) after Kali uses the well-lit bathroom and, as always, dances with her mom in the wall-length mirror to the tastefully selected music overhead. That night, we get burritos and watch an animated movie back home. This is how we live our life.

Inner

Mission

I'd thought I heard some **structural creaking** *overhead between sets,*

the air misty with something

more noxious than psychoactive smoke.

It wasn't entirely surprising, therefore,

that the roof of the arena seemed

breached.

No shitstorms

forecasted for New York City that night,

as far as I knew, and although earlier in the day

I once or twice had whiffed that old familiar stench,

no event approaching such enormous sloppiness,

such

momentous

untidiness,

such godawful

olfactory

intrusion,

had seemed imminent.

But it's undeniable now . . .

The roof of the Garden had

c r a c k e d

o p e n !

Holy

fucking

excrement

raining

down

Everyone revels in it,

smears it,

slips in it,

and then,

on their backs,

they

flap

arms

and

scissor

legs

until angels appear in the aisles that stand to dance,

laughing all the way,

full-on coprophagous grins

on every face,

laughing
and
laughing
until
they

f   a   l   l   a   p   a   r   t   .

"when you're taking a piece of energy, at a fast, a huge, an incredible, y'know, a *high speed*, it's like physics, y'know, the faster, the faster you go the rounder you get, y'know, the faster you go in the fourth dimension, y'know, the *bigger you get*, so as a thing approaches light, the speed of light, it gains mass, right? Okay, and that's it, uh, and that's like, so when you're talking about energy in the history, *the fast-moving history stream*, when you stick something out in there, it's gaining energy, it's gaining momentum at the rate of *the time flow*, so to speak, and now things are going fast, so for example, well, consider how much, how much *weight* The Beatles put out there, or Bob Dylan, y'know what I mean, or, uh, Herman Hesse, or, uh, y'know, *anybody* who's stuck their head up in this last century. *BAM!* Y'know so if you put a *lie* out there, y'know, and it accumulates energy, what you've got is, y'know, y'know, well, we're living in a state of lies gone, y'know, accumulating vast energy, y'know, and, and, the result is, the incredible *chaos* that faces civilization."

—Jerry Garcia

Our six-year-old daughter knows where I'm going when I leave for the train. You'll get synesthesia? she says. I'll see sounds, I say, hear colors, feel them both if all goes well, and regardless, no matter what happens, honey, it'll all smell a lot like weed. I don't say that last part as I leave Mamou and Kali with my mother and her big old black Labrador retriever at my childhood home in west-central New Jersey and hurry for a train leaving in twenty minutes. Seconds later I pass two massive Picasso-like heads along the highway and swing the car toward the train station that shares an exit with the sculpture park, expecting to zip into the garage and make the train with time to spare. But there's a line of cars out to the access road. The garage must be full. Cars turn around and speed along station roads to get five spots ahead of where they were, aggressively merging into the line directed into a parking lot. Eight bucks, no overnight. I have a ten. They say it's OK if I don't return until three, that's not overnight.

The train before the one I thought I'd catch has been sitting at the station a while, might as well jump on, the doors still open, expecting once seated to write on my phone about the previous day seeing my dad at his memory-care facility before visiting the Rhombus, not wanting to bring a book, not sure I can bring a book into the Garden, don't want to worry about it falling from my jacket pocket, the day warm and clear so not wearing my coat, a sunny Saturday four days before New Year's Eve, December 28, 2019 to be exact, at about 10:15 in the morning, as I step onto the train.

It's standing room only. I lean against a plastic divider by the door, content when the train starts moving to watch woods whirl by. Near me, a family speaks such rapid Spanish I can only make out a few words. They're laughing about a photo on the young father's phone of one of the women, his wife I guess, mother of some or all of the kids with them. She playfully hits him and shows me the picture, says in a thick accent her husband doesn't respect her. In the picture her hair's a mess, she wears a robe and sweatpants and furry slippers. I say you clean up nice, unwilling to speak Spanish, wanting to preserve eavesdropper status for our hour on the train together.

Incoming passengers propel the family to the upper deck. A youngish Black guy with dreads and a nose ring squeezes on. We're pressed together by an Asian family and an older white guy in a FedEx hat. There's a smell of weed so strong I can taste it through my strawberry gum. Soon enough the dreadlocked guy's telling me about his skateboarding career, showing me his Instagram (@darth.dinero). His cheeks are rounded and loose, his eyes pacific, his speech inflected by stoner skater culture. He's injured now, almost thirty, but he was sponsored by a company I haven't heard of, neither Powell Peralta nor Sims.

We talk about early '70s Southern California skaters, that documentary with the great soundtrack, Hendrix instead of Suicidal Tendencies since skate punk wasn't around yet. I listened to but was never all that into those mid-'80s bands, JFA, Circle Jerks, Dead Kennedys, the Repo Man soundtrack, at most could do a 360 and jump a curb. I was better at catamaraning, starting with a friend at the top of a hill, sitting on our boards, facing one another with boards parallel, heels on either side of the other board, shifting weight to direct us down the hill, like tandem sledding down sloped blacktop. Not much of a maneuver but fun if you can't skate well.

Now we catamaran toward the city, the gently rocking train floor our board, questions and responses how we direct the flow, even if it's asymmetrical, inequivalent as we lean to the left, tilt to the right. He asks no questions but then again I was never sponsored.

I can't quite remember the name of that skater documentary. Loved it so much after renting it one night I watched it again with coffee in the morning, how those surfer kids started in drained pools before it evolved to half-pipes, ramps, and skate parks, revolutionizing skateboarding from gentle slaloming on flat ground, with competitions more like dog shows, prancing on wheels.

He says the name of the movie is "Lords of Dogtown," and I say but that's the movie, right? What was the documentary? Something like Dogtown Z Boys?

Dogtown *and* Z Boys, states Darth Dinero.

The documentary was better, I say, and he agrees, and it seems like something's developing about the representation of fact as fact or fact as fiction.

Valuing the documentary over the movie activates a binary.

I say to myself something like *uh ight now it's on*, saluting the emergence of theme, deeming it validation of the technique I'll use to describe the day chosen in advance once I bought a ticket for a concert on December 28 at the Garden.

I would take notes for a long story/short novel about a single day, structured in time by the trip to the city, the time before the show, the show itself, and the trip home, the show's temporal approach and progress creating *narrative drive* as they say. But the real show would be the day itself. And now en route from suburban New Jersey to New York City on December 28, 2019, Darth Dinero and I value documentary over drama.

A young Asian woman reviews apartments for sale on her phone. She seems two feet shorter than me, wearing a white puffy coat with a furry hood, immersed in her oversized screen, which I can see without making an effort from far overhead. The apartments all seem like they're in the twenties and thirties of Manhattan, close to our destination, all of them white walled, huge windows displaying bright blue skies, each property well over a million dollars, three hundred square feet shot to seem airy, spacious, the walls at oblique angles, the light suggestive of Greece. I hope they're heading into the city to buy an apartment for her, very exciting, or they're going in for any other reason and she removes herself, fantasizing about a million-dollar studio apartment of her own.

To my right, a group of young white women occupy the area in front of the north door. One woman in particular wears a Patriots winter cap over blond hair and soft pale face. It seems like she's had perioral cosmetic surgery involving marshmallow instead of collagen. She says there's a flu epidemic in Times Square. A friend went there before Christmas and came home super-sick, everyone who goes there comes back sick, two to three days later they're deathly ill.

Ever since they sanitized Times Square all the filth leapt into the air. XXX theaters and ramshackle outlets selling naughty mags and fake IDs epitomized sickness itself. Sanitized tourists stayed away and so never returned from Times Square sick but now they flock there for Broadway shows and enormous electronic advertisements up the sides of skyscrapers, thinking it family-friendly and safe. It's more likely now that someone coughs on their hand and touches a railing and so on. But I prefer to think of the sickness that comes on three days later as the ghost of Times Square's past.

It was Christmas a few days ago, the influx of everything festive, tree, decorations, presents, wrapping paper, relatives, alimentation and alcohol in excess, holiday programming, all of it making me more susceptible to sickness. I wonder if spending time at the Garden with nineteen thousand people will expose me to that flu. I'm sure hundreds will visit Times Square before the show—in town for the first time, it's nearby, they want to see it, upload a sweet panorama to Instagram—and at one point they touch the offending effluvia.

Darth Dinero responds enthusiastically in the affirmative to a question about his preference for skiing or snowboarding. He grew up in north-central New Jersey and was enrolled in a program where he was bused daily to slopes in southern New York for intensive snowboarding practice. He was sponsored by Burton, the only snowboard company I could name, but lost the sponsorship as he aged. He says he filmed a reel that wasn't up to par.

Darth Dinero has seen better days. Pushing thirty, knee recovering from injury, going to work at an AT&T store in Newark late on a Saturday morning.

More than twenty years ago, for six weeks in the summer, I regularly got off at Newark Penn Station to switch to the Newark subway, which I remember being 100% more wooden than any other train I'd been on in the United States. It also had windows that opened, and once it wasn't running because it had caught on fire. I took it to assist in a summer program for incoming first-year students at the New Jersey Institute of Technology, where a neighbor of my parents headed the English Literature department.

Both my parents had lived in Newark until the mid-1960s, my father in the Weequahic neighborhood, about ten years younger than Philip Roth, who set so many of his novels there, who I've used as a guide to what it was like,

my father not one to talk about growing up in Newark beyond saying he preferred sandlot baseball to Saturday syn-
agogue or mentioning that his parents moved to Union a
few years before the riots after they were sitting in their
living room when an arm came through an open window,
trying to snag a wallet left on a table.

My mother grew up in what's now called the Iron-
bound, a poor neighborhood filled with drunks, lunatics,
perverts, as she describes it, before the Portuguese arrived.
Without Philip Roth I wouldn't have a sense of the city,
and I still don't, not really, although when there I feel a
connection to it as the place where my grandparents lived
most of their lives, my paternal grandfather born in 1902
never once traveling the handful of miles by rail or road
to Manhattan, never considering it, whereas my father as a
kid would go to Brooklyn to see the Dodgers, a cinematic
adventure, early 1950s, sepia-toned and slightly sped up.

A family gets on at Newark Airport with a newborn in
a stroller. Everyone jostles and makes room even if making
more room seemed impossible minutes ago. A pink-haired
woman pushes through, freaking, looking for a bathroom.
She's either having a panic attack or really needs to pee.
Otherwise it's been the most cordial, severely packed train
ride imaginable, friendly conversation among strangers
throughout.

New Jersey Transit to New York City, a few dozen miles
east of Philadelphia, it's a different culture. After thirteen
years in Philadelphia and six recent months riding the
quiet car to and from its southwestern suburbs, waiting for

it each way, I'm accustomed to universal observation of silence and polite tolerance of the presence of other people, something that at first dispirited me, how everyone's so protective and respectful of privacy, unwilling to divulge or pry. Most seem never to look up, certainly not at another person. At most a quick glance and then at their phone or into the distance, whereas in NYC and even this train, an extension of the city, people look at people, hold glances an extended second, judge, determine, imagine.

In the Philadelphia area I've felt like some gawking neurotic weirdo for looking at people, the way now on the train to New York I look at two older white gentlemen to my right: a father in his eighties, a son in his sixties, seated, reading German newspapers, wearing fine sweaters, somewhat unkempt as though they didn't shower this morning, Euro-tinted eyeglasses, glancing at me and Darth Dinero and others, exchanging quiet phrases in German. Their presence, sitting with backs to the train's north-side windows, seems calming, or at least they do nothing to agitate fellow passengers, unlike the Jewishy middle-aged plaster-complexioned guy on the train's south side, to my left, a few years older than me I reckon, in Federal Express hat and matching hooded sweatshirt, pressed against the tall narrow window of the sliding door, repeating that the train's packed because of "freebies."

My peripheral hearing registers the word *freebies* roughly five dozen times. *Freebies, freebies, freebies, freebies, freebies, freebies, freebies, freebies, freebies, freebies, freebies, freebies, freebies, freebies.* I don't quite listen to his explanation about a compounding effect of conductors not taking tickets and riders not activating tickets on their apps, so everyone now has multiple tickets on their phones that don't expire until 2034.

I look for the right moment to extend a disembarking gift to Darth Dinero as we approach Newark. As he starts to exit I say here's something to ward off that nasty flu. It's not that strong but it's effective. It'll keep you *in da couch.*

I say something cryptic and weird like that as I offer a candy wrapped in cellophane to a stranger on a train.

Darth Dinero says thanks bro that's tight. He receives it in a way that makes it clear he's practiced in the art of clandestine handovers and knows what I'm handing him, especially when I suggest he should wait until after work to eat it.

Not sure why I wanted to share my limited stash with him, beyond perceived connection based on demeanor and scent. I had a pre-rolled joint a friend in Denver had mailed to me as a housewarming present after our move in June, two quarters of a 100-gram gummy purchased the last time I played at the South Philly practice space with my septuagenarian drummer friend, and two hard candies presumably infused with 10 grams of indica, also a gift from a good old friend (Crow) who since his move to California a few years ago bestows upon me a baggie of gummies whenever he visits the home area. It's more than enough for the show of course, plus vape pens and whatever will make the rounds as usual during the concert, everyone intent on elation, alleviation, immersion in a sonic substance bound by time that the band somehow makes timeless, unbounded by song structure or melody or recognizable motif other than the sound the band makes when doing what they and really only they do: collapse or expand or obviate or suspend the regular experience of time. "This will inoculate you from the Times Square flu" is another way of putting it, a euphemism for the temporary suspension of everything awful, a vestigial gesture of Yuletide cheer, the multitudes saying glory to God, good will to all.

It was Christmas three days ago but New Year's Eve three days from now pulls stronger, a final indulgence before refreshing January starkness. The holiday season I now understand as blowout indulgence/extravagance to get us through darkest days. Removal of all that crap lets us appreciate the lack of stockings hanging with care. The space where the tree stood now freed and the chair placed there again when I sit in the morning with my laptop before catching the 5:34 train. Gummy inoculation from Times Square normies. Something like that. I just wanted to slip him something on a packed train, not really caring if anyone registered it, not yet accustomed to the idea it's nearly legal in New Jersey and New York, something I'll never get my head around thanks to the "Just Say No" and "This Is Your Brain on Drugs" propaganda of my teens, when I was most apt to scramble the eggs of perception.

Quasi-illegal action maybe felt necessary to separate December 28, 2019 from daily good deeds, a break from everyday life as a good boy, working well, waking at 4:45 for the 5:34 train, getting everything done, preparing nourishing meals, rarely anything more processed than rice or pasta I taste to ensure it's done but otherwise don't eat, although lately liable to order a Friday night pizza when exhausted, what I consider being "bad." The extent of my transgression: reading and drinking two beers at a bar in town before walking home and calling for a pizza I then drive to pick up, sometimes with Kali strapped in the car seat behind me, not at all buzzed by the time it's time to get the pizza. Living on the edge.

The bars in town: the large regional brewery chain usually has a spot to sit and happy-hour specials on adequate watery craft beer. Its long bar where you sit with your back to the room, facing the brewing vats, makes it hard to see anyone, so I keep my glasses on and read. There's a more expensive place down the street that seems constructed of Lincoln Logs with the worst music in the world (Rod Stewart ballads). There's also a half-circle of a bar with libertarian-type quotations on the walls and a sense I shouldn't sit there and read. Or there's a narrow dark bar with dozens of screens offering every flavor of ESPN and as many taps, where after informing the bartender that their music beat the competition's by miles he said these days he pretty much only listens to one band. I said as a matter of fact I have a ticket for the first night of that band's four-show New Year's run at the Garden, and then we talked about our chances of winning a ticket for the free show sponsored by SiriusXM at a renovated opera house on Broad Street on December 3, 2019. We both ultimately won tickets but I haven't been back to discuss that show or the bartender's trip to his hometown Pittsburgh for the December 4 show, one I listened to and envied.

On Fridays I explore the town after work, in part to get a sense of the locals, the regulars, the way in South Philly I knew the faces of those who lived at the two bars I attended with any frequency. I missed the familiarity, even if I remember no names now, but over a dozen years we greeted one another when we passed in Center City but not in the bar itself, where I felt comfortable reading while drinking half-off happy hour beers as good music played (too much Motörhead maybe). It was an extension of home, same as the smaller, newer, and for me better place around the corner that played vinyl, almost too often selecting Can's "Tago Mago."

They played John Cale's "Paris 1919" one afternoon. I'd never heard it, was blown away, asked about it, acquired it on vinyl after a thousand streams. This may seem meaningless but introduction to a previously unknown masterpiece like John Cale's "Paris 1919" supports existence in that it's an increasingly rare instance of the appearance, the *apparition,* of beauty. It's more than that, really. It's reinforcement of the little cocktail umbrella I hold above my head to ward off the storm of shit.

[NOTE TO READER: THE "SOUNDCHECK" TEXT CURRENTLY ON PAGE 3 ORIGINALLY APPEARED HERE AND WAS EXCERPTED AND MOVED UPFRONT FOR REASONS OF THEMATIC ESTABLISHMENT AND ENTICE- MENT OF READERS LURED BY REFERENCE

TO THE LAST LINE IN ROBERTO BOLAÑO'S
BY NIGHT IN CHILE]

My departing gift to Darth Dinero as he exits the train acknowledges enthusiasm we share for sheltering beneath the wings of a certain psychoactive. Everything about Darth Dinero reeked to the point that in his vicinity his single most observable characteristic was Total Stoner. And as a total stoner during foundational identity-formation years the gifted gummy recognizes the shared subtype, as sacrament and secret handshake, common ground and connection with a stranger.

Not sure why I overcomplicate a train ride into New York City on a late Saturday morning four nights before New Year's 2019-2020, this so-called *irrelevant* event of a ride on a packed train across New Jersey to New York City, the corridor between Philadelphia and New York apparently the most densely populated extended stretch in the world, the heart of Bos-Wash, its waist at least, the center of it. It's an impossible and therefore beautiful task to describe one day in any detail, textual reanimation of the filaments of life.

The train's not as packed after Newark. The tunnel into Manhattan, the windows go dark, the excitement of imminent dispersal, packed together for a time and then off in our own directions. I talk with a middle-aged white woman, maybe five or ten years older than me, maybe my age. She agrees with an abundance of cheer that it's been a cheerful train ride, could have been worse, only that pink-haired woman freaked out, everyone's been friendly, content, chatty, social, unexpectedly so. It felt like an event, no use suffering through it, everyone energized to get out of the house after the holiday, everyone with plans in the city, sun's shining, warm for late December, in the fifties, among the darkest days but radiant, breezy, clear.

She stands closer to the front of the train than where I stand. To her left, sitting on the row of seats beneath the south-side windows, there's a younger Black couple. The man wears designer sunglasses and a form-fitting Gucci sweatshirt. His pecs seem alive. His chest moves on its own, the strength there not at rest as we travel through the tunnel. I'd faced the opposite direction the whole ride, no idea who was behind me, unaware of my surroundings. Not that I need to see everything but my eyes are peeled, as we say with Kali, alert to whatever the day has in mind.

I ascend a flight of stairs behind the FedEx Freebies guy. Stonewashed jeans, white-leather sneakers, about my age, a little older. Is that what I look like, despite darker jeans and more stylish sneakers? Indistinguishable from other middle-aged white guys, not exactly bounding up these steps?

A momentarily disorientating entrance into Penn Station proper, unsure where I find myself. Ticket windows. A somewhat unfamiliar and what I would call *new* although probably ten-year-old section lively with travelers. Most seem younger. A tall young white male reading Murakami's *1Q84*. I haven't read any Murakami novels and imagine a year in the immediate future reading everything he's written in order of publication. Already the city influencing me, going to work on my reading list.

Before I take the train to Brooklyn I should relieve myself. I negotiate through billowing streams of anarchic human movement, scanning for a tell-tale T-shirt or winter hat with red donut design (the band's unofficial logo, matching the pattern on the drummer's dress), looking for someone with the same plans, also inspecting the station for changes. The pizza place still there, Krispy Kreme. The bathroom still in the same spot. It's guarded. Always someone shaving at one of the many sinks, always someone wearing dark sunglasses, trench coat, platform boots. Tunnel vision to a urinal, familiar with the place, focused on relief, the orderly anarchy of a micturitive assembly line, everyone aware and unaware of everyone else.

The sinks were updated since last time here. Burnished silver fixtures, the lighting not harsh as expected but emitted from either side of the mirror in such a way that makes your eyes seem to glow, water activated by motion sensors. Sudden awareness it's almost 2020, even Penn Station's men's room seems designed and slick, beyond functional, beyond reasonable expectation. Someone made it their business to ensure that everyone streaming through this bathroom emerges impressed with the extravagance and likely expense. Such a moment in their lives will marginally improve everyone's days and therefore as a consequence improve the days of thousands, possibly millions, in the city and throughout the world since surely so many mornings involve these sinks before taking the train to Newark Airport or a car to La Guardia or JFK. Pleasing bathroom sink experience intended to achieve positive international ripple effect seems indicative of the current city. Traditional expectation reversed, grit replaced by grace, a degree of danger and outright indigent stank now safe and sanitized opulence. Nothing simply functional or accidental. Everything seems *determined*, quantified for maximum positive impact on the shared urban environment.

Directly to the left when leaving the bathroom there's a TGIFridays (which I always call TGIF Friday's) where Mamou once found a wad of cash. Like some lifeless parrot it was just kinda splayed on the floor a few steps inside. She picked it up, counted it ($200+), and then gave it to the bartender in case someone came in claiming to have lost a stack of cash. The bartender, thankful she proved herself such a good citizen and did the right thing, said he was willing to hold onto it. I would have pocketed it and only handed it over if someone in obvious need ran in, wrecked about the missing money.

It's New York! It's Penn Station! A random wad of cash!

Mamou ultimately said the bartenders could split it if no one came in asking for it, sure they'd hand it over if anyone inquired . . .

Another night there alone waiting for a train back to Philadelphia, watching basketball, the bartender mentioned they do their best business when the band's playing the Garden, everyone packs the place and tips well. An older man next to me, bald except on the sides, overgrown mustache, professorial, in my memory the spitting image of Kurt Vonnegut, asked what they sound like?

The bartender said they're a jam band.

Vonnegut said like Steely Dan?

I said more like a cross between Zappa and the Grateful Dead, with some Peter Gabriel-era Genesis, Talking Heads, Little Feat, and Ween mixed in there, huge jams but with silly, playful lyrics, and long, intricate, composed, almost classical, sometimes cartoonish parts that sound unlike anyone else.

So like Steely Dan, said Vonnegut.

No, I said, not really, you can hear influences but everything ultimately sounds like them. Bluegrass, a cappella barbershop, Zeppelin covers, a complicated original song where the lyrics are just "David Bowie, David Bowie, UB40, UB40," not silky sleek jazzy urban-cool irony like Steely Dan.

I hadn't listened to them in years but maintained a fondness and could still access the excitement of hearing them for the first time, second or third weekend at college when I drank too much with a sophomore Deadhead (bearded, overweight, Northfield Mt. Hermon graduate, often wore a batik tapestry as a sort of housedress, showed me a purely textual, nascent form of the internet on his computer) who played a cassette of the band's visit to the college in April 1990, the semester before I'd arrived. He dubbed that and a few others for me and I listened to them a hundred times before they returned on April 18, 1991. The ticket cost $7. I stood fifteen feet from the bass player, had more than enough room to flail, felt like liquid mercury knocked around by virtuoso players of some postmodern pinball machine. Classical bits transformed into cartoon chase scenes followed by soaring heroic crescendos based on two chords like Coltrane, The Allmans, The Dead, and now . . . this, whatever *this* was?

I'd been playing guitar for three years and was getting passable but the guitarist played the way I would play if I had the next hundred years free to practice. The way writers reveal what readers have always thought but never put into words, the guitarist's playing seemed so fun, clear and creative, easy to follow down unpredictable paths, *gnarly*, awesome, rippin', ridiculous, *just fucking great*. What my friends at the time called *sickness* (the supreme accolade). A master at building tension and maximizing release. I came away from that first show more than a little in love. I was nineteen, twenty-eight years ago, and the band's still at it, a ticket in my pocket (purchased from StubHub for $211.19 including taxes, fees, and Fed-Ex'ing the official *objet d'art* paper ticket to our new-ish home) to see them tonight in the upper deck of "the world's most famous arena" as I negotiate waves of foot traffic.

Twenty years ago when I worked from a room in a shared Greenpoint apartment I reverse commuted, leaving the house as everyone headed home, after a day alone inside at a desktop computer, clunky old beige monitor with a plastic dinosaur figurine atop it, a sea monster with a long neck that shook during a 2.0 earthquake right down Broadway one morning, foreshadowing Lower Manhattan catastrophe a year later. I'd walk to the Bedford L against the current of everyone returning home, get out at First Avenue and walk north through the Gramercy and Murray Hill, an acquisitive march across miles organized into blocks, making it to the park before heading back on the west side to the 8th Avenue L stop, home hours later.

I haven't been to the Garden since I was six or seven, upper deck, for the Ringling Brothers and Barnum & Bailey Circus, little plastic lights on strings kids spun around, elephants, tightrope walkers, the commemorative poster's old-timey script like on the bullfight poster I got around that time with my parents in Spain, the first excursions, to NYC and another country, experiences reduced to souvenirs pinned to bedroom wall. *Bravos toros* = brave bulls.

I won't buy a poster for the show tonight, won't get a T-shirt, will keep my ticket stub since it's issued from the band and not a generic Ticketmaster production or a screenshot of a StubHub barcode on my phone. The mp3s will be available for free download the next day from the band's site, which I'll listen to at work several times, trying to find something more in the music than I heard the moment it was played.

Emergence into form may be what I'm attracted to, why I want to be there, the way the show I saw at the Mann Music Center in Philadelphia, August 12, 2015, now sounds composed after multiple listens, but at the time, with low expectations, the sound *exploded* toward me, *rushed* me. I was primed for it, energetic, in late-summer shape, able to keep up, move with it, fluid and flexible and strong, responsive and in sync, the way the lights move with the band as though choreographed.

Not since the early '90s seeing the band at small clubs and theaters, or the Dead and JGB wherever, had I had that experience. Some bands approached it but there was always a distance, even if standing close to the front, aware I blocked the view. Even five rows back it was never the same as with no one else between me and the music.

At that summer amphitheater show in 2015 I was separated from friends and so found myself alone in a sea of joyous undulation on a clear warm midweek night. Almost five years later, it's noon on a Saturday toward the end of 2019, an arena show, upper deck seats, I don't feel as well, in seasonal decline, but it's guaranteed to sound good, and I'll write about it regardless, the night selected in advance.

I should conserve step count but of course decide to walk instead of take a downtown A, B, or C to 14th and then switch to the L to Union Square to switch to a Brooklyn-bound Q. The southwestern escalator, flu epidemic burbling on the ever-ascending conveyor-belt railing, I risk it for an easy climb, otherwise standing still. And at the top it's the classic meatstick cart always at the corner of Thirty-Second Street and Eighth Avenue, the sight and smell and sound of *New York City*. In seven hours I'll be back to enter the Garden, no one waiting outside now, no trace of a Shakedown.

I usually walk down Eighth toward Chelsea galleries for the city's free art shows before heading downtown or to Brooklyn but now I just try to stay in the sun, acclimate to foot traffic, the blurred whirl at an ambulatory 3 MPH, reminded at once how men in these parts seem to sometimes impede progress a moment to assert their existence. I try not to look too closely at anyone while not missing anyone, every pedestrian representative.

I stop to take a photo of over-earnest political commentary on a wall near a bus stop. A woman like Shelley Duvall, tall and thin with silver dollar eyes, bags under them, gym clothes, turns a corner and looks at me in a way I'm no longer accustomed to, more like she's checking her status than checking me out, gauging the duration of my glance.

Overthinking momentary pedestrian interactions, once again experiencing sidewalk traffic, passersby. The Chelsea Hotel. A nearby bar where I met a friend I no longer talk to, a video artist who tried to convince me to move back after my first year in Philadelphia before he got into yoga with his girlfriend and moved upstate.

I only lived here four years, four years that felt much longer, not wanting to retell the story and further reduce it. I've retold it to nothing twenty years later, now more a memory of its retelling, the dream of everything that happened there dispelled. The first times I retold it to friends at grad school in booths at bars they were engaged, eyes focused on improbable internet-addled romance with a well-known young writer from London, sad inevitable end followed a month later by watching the Towers fall from the

Williamsburg Bridge, and then winding up in a new relationship with another writer I knew from college, half-Jew like me, from Manhattan but now lived in Iowa City where I moved for the Writers' Workshop where I retold the story to new friends.

It sounds like someone else's life now, the first love interest regularly publishing novels, essay collections, a story collection recently. I no longer read them as soon as they're published, an eye out for a nod to me. Downtown, I wonder if I'll run into her, but not much between Penn Station and Union Square exists on the nostalgia continuum.

Everything's been hosed down, the streets at least, whereas the sidewalks seem dusty and salt-stained. An old woman with a grocery cart takes up the entire sidewalk, talking to an old man wearing a sweatshirt with "I'm not yelling, I'm Armenian" printed across the chest. He spits a dollop of murk to the curb as I step around them. Banks everywhere, as expected. I move like a predator more than a pedestrian as though I'm not a tourist even though I haven't been here in almost two years other than holiday parties for work, bused up the Turnpike and through the tunnel, the skyline changed since I was a kid on school trips craning for first sight of the Twin Towers, or when in the car with my mother when she'd drag me to SoHo galleries before lunch at the Cupping Room or Le Petit Cafe where the sandwiches seemed dainty and expensive.

At the corner of the street that intersects the western side of Union Square there used to be a popular diner/bar, currently undergoing conversion into a bank. The seafood restaurant across the street where I went with the writer from London and her publishing team after a packed Barnes and Noble reading, defending her when her publicist said something condescending about the writer's perfume and then smoking a cigarette at the bar, back when you could still smoke in bars even when they adjoined restaurants. That place closed too, not yet converted into a Duane Reade or Citibank, each block's endgame until some inevitable devastation starts the process anew.

The light in Union Square seems dramatic, chill, primaveral, blanching the farmers' market and making it seem staged but improvised, real if nowhere near raw. The Virgin Megastore no longer streaming dry ice smoke from some fissure in its facade, where the writer from London, browsing compact discs, was approached by a scout for a serious modeling firm, one she'd heard of. Given a business card, saying she had the look they were looking for, the look of the future, she said she already had a decent job as a novelist, thank you, but as a formerly overweight mixed-race ugly duckling, always reading, wearing chunky glasses and oversized jumpers, being approached in her mid-twenties by a legit modeling scout seemed like good news.

The Whole Foods Market, a Hari Krishna, the Ulysses S. Grant equestrian statue. Rallies there after 9/11 seemed spontaneous. Posters for the lost. The city I'd lived in at a dramatic time, twenty years later dramatically reconfigured. First impressions imprinted as though they'd always been that way. CBGBs wasn't always there. St. Marks and the Bowery weren't always how they'd seemed when I first walked down them. SoHo in the fifties, sixties, seventies, eighties, nineties, oughts, now. And that's not even touching on Williamsburg and Greenpoint, warehouses razed, condos along the river, empty lots no longer empty, Astro-Turf on the McCarren Park soccer field the metonymic representative.

Always fun to buy a MetroCard, the game how fast you process the touchscreen interface, the card emitted at pace. I want to stay present but the past is always there, remembering a kid flying through the menu, fast-talking some private sign language with the machine.

I'll take the Q to Ditmas Park to meet an old friend at his mother's apartment. The platform seems subterranean: stalactites and stalagmites should have formed in crevices untroubled by trains. It's almost humid as though the walls of the cave perform a pulmonary function. Good subway karma, train arrives without wait, and at the Q train door I meet FedEx Freebies from the New Jersey Transit train.

I say something like *wow, hey, incredible*, we were feet from each other on the train into the city and now here we are, walking through the same door of the Q.

The end of the car where we enter is empty. He sits opposite me and we talk about the train into the city. He explains what he meant by "freebies," how they stopped checking tickets on packed trains so trains became progressively packed, on weekends especially, everyone with multiple old unused tickets on their phones. Now since everyone knows trains will be too packed to check tickets, everyone gets on without tickets. All of which is what he meant by *freebies*.

His eyes never pause to focus on a single point. There's a philosophical glee to everything he says, a humor, even if what he says as he lectures about the subway system, for example, isn't funny at all.

It's 125 years old and needs urgent care, he says, his grin stretching the folds of his pasty white cheeks.

My dad's seventy seven and not doing well, I say, so I imagine a subway system fifty years older could use some work.

He lauds the Los Angeles subway. Newer systems are so much better but have nowhere near the ridership.

I say *but seriously isn't it crazy* we were feet from each other on the train into the city, everyone went separate ways for half an hour, and then we walked through *the same door* of the Q?

He says to be honest I don't remember you from the train, lots of people on it.

I say you got on at Metuchen, and he corrects me and says Elizabeth.

I say *I'm sure* it was Metuchen, and he says *I'm sure* I got on at Elizabeth.

I say there was an Asian family next to you.

He says *yeah sure* I remember them but I didn't see you.

I say *how could you not have seen me?* I was standing five feet from you next to that dreadlocked dude for like half an hour.

He says I remember the guy with the dreadlocks, I guess I just didn't notice you.

I say *so just now*, at the door of the subway, when I said *WOW HEY AMAZING*, you had no idea what I was talking about?

No idea, he says.

I cross my arms and stretch my legs, exaggeratedly exasperated, performing an off-put Seinfeldian pantomime as the train hurtles under the river and emerges in Brooklyn, the elevated airy path through the borough.

I thumb notes into my phone, what's occurred so far, as FedEx Freebies gets some shut eye. I consult my maps app, concerned about battery drain, trying to figure out where to go once I get off at Conselyea. Wrong direction if I see a Duane Reade.

Ahead on the platform is guy who looks like he could be Kiko, wearing all black, black Converses, a small potted flowering plant upright on either palm, the way a waiter balances platters. Everywhere there's color and movement. Everything deserves a moment's focus, peripheral color and movement shift as I focus on a blurred floral sense across the tracks.

Every morning when I walk to the train, when I walk through underground passages from 11th to 6th Street, it's still night when I walk to my office at the corner of 4th and Market, everything beige and white and gray, the carpeting in the long hallway to the kitchen a muddy green. In my office I keep the lights off, the only colors on my computer screen. I got an iPad three days before the trip to New York, played with a drawing app, impressed with the colors, unaware I've been in a color-depleted state until the open subway platform at Conselyea Street, the guy ahead of me walking toward the exit held two flowering plants on his palms, the brilliance of which somehow extended to advertisements and winter coats and hats and faces, walls spray-painted in vermillion graffiti, whatever else.

At street level, walking on the shady side, it seems different than the day before Kiko's wedding, October 2012. Brunch places, wine stores, boutiques mixed in with the bodegas, West Indian restaurants, tagged shuttered storefronts I remember. Enlightened multicultural paradise is the impression but I'm sure it's all struggle and strife before displacement for condos, convenience-store pharmacies, banks.

Every block seems endangered the way open spaces in west-central New Jersey when I was growing up seemed like sites for inevitable archaeological digs. Massive yellow backhoes would excavate the future, unearthing Toll Brothers homes concealed beneath scrappy woods and corn fields. Where my mother now lives alone, still in the same home they bought fifty years ago, every acre is either developed or protected, the chance of change reduced to zero. But the city seems in constant flux, radical physical and demographic change always in play until a Citibank occupies street level below an aerial expanse of glass, symbolic parallel for the end of individuation, every individual a city block, all idiosyncrasies dissolved by death. ☺

I see Kiko ahead on a block lined by a brick wall. He kicks his heels, looks at his phone, strolls nowhere in winding slow motion. Narrow in a waist-length jacket, he looks more like a torero than a waiter, less lion than ocelot. I pull my old down jacket over my head and walk toward him, hiding, although who else would walk right at him, face concealed by jacket? We hug like old college friends, now twenty-five years since graduation, almost thirty since we met, Kiko on the same floor as the room I shared with my roommate, both arrived early for soccer preseason, Kiko with incredible long hair, veiny arms and legs, light brown skin, lithe, his athleticism an afterthought of youth. Christ-like, casually beatific, unconcerned with cool, graceful yet spastic, not at all into the music I brought to college, didn't habitually smoke weed, a force of nature not interested in being a force.

He showed me his first paper for an English Lit class. It was called "my eyes are larger than yours." He'd drawn eyes on it. It was an incomprehensible prose poem in which he approached the assignment from an abstract angle. He was overflowing with creative energy, and I took it upon myself to white man him, contain his flow, translate rangy idiosyncratic abstraction into something academically acceptable.

No better time than first year in college to eff the ineffable: his approach was a homemade poetics that led to art and religion classes, a semester in India, cross-legged sensitive conversations with womyn almost his equal in terms of impressive healthy locks. By senior year he'd cut his hair and grown a beard, and after college worked at Chicago galleries putting up temporary walls, building crates to ship art. Helped build John McEntire's studio at Damon and Division, played on an indoor soccer team ("Raisin Lungs") with members of June of '44, Jim O'Rourke bought him a beer on his birthday at The Empty Bottle. Moved back to his home state of Texas, to Marfa, bought a place with his Kiwi girlfriend, a curator, and then moved to Brooklyn when she went to grad school upstate somewhere, followed by a temporary curatorial position at a prestigious midtown museum. Now he works at a major Chelsea gallery, preparing work for private viewings for prospective buyers.

In college, after he returned from India, he had a small notebook filled with impressive, intricate, not-quite-symmetrical drawings of bull skulls. He could draw but wasn't driven to do it. He always had a super-creative spirit even if he didn't create. It wasn't rare by the time we reached our thirties for creative friends not to create. Everyone had seemed creative in college but few practiced anything in particular over time, rarely committed to developing skill beyond initial facility.

He'd married the Kiwi curator and had a daughter now five years old. I was excited to meet her again although I'd seen pictures and had visited the apartment they'd had in Red Hook (two doors down from a grad school friend's apartment) a few years before when she was a few months old. My destination is an enormous room with nineteen thousand people but first Kiko leads me to his mother's apartment on the first floor of a pleasant apartment building not far from the corner where we met.

Kiko's mother had taught Spanish in Klein, Texas. I'd always found it odd that my surname was the same as Kiko's school district. They'd lived in a suburb of Houston, which when I visited before he and I went to Mexico in January 1992, had seemed unlike any city I'd ever seen. Highways leading to tall buildings where no one lived, detention basins to prevent flooding, strip malls maybe at most. I only really remember streets lined with live oaks near Rice University and the Rothko Museum. Kiko's mother suggested that he and I cut our hair before going to Mexico since hair to the middle of our backs would attract police and thieves. We of course were idealistic, thinking it'd attract people who might want to help us or show us cool things or get us high. I definitely was interested in the latter; Kiko not so much. His father, born in Northern Ireland, had learned to read Mayan glyphs while living in Mexico, where he'd met Kiko's future mother, and eventually in Houston made a living as a piano tuner. He often stopped at a bar after work and had trouble leaving or would drive his car off the road and park it there until he sobered enough to make it home. When Kiko drank or smoked, whenever he lost some control, he associated it with his father, a heaviness overtook him, soon enough he became bleary, dreary, moody, saturnine, and worked his way back to his preferred state of sobriety.

Kiko's mother is small and solid, wearing a long fuzzy sweater that accentuates a cute squatness and, with short curls and round face, makes her seem like a wise little owl. A widow since the mid-'90s. Sold the family home in Texas and moved near daughter and son in Brooklyn, the whole family in Ditmas Park. The apartment is an open kitchen, living room, dining room combo and a bedroom. Their suburban Houston home, its yard and landscaping, everything cedarish, vaguely Asian, sagging blue-gray evergreens and low polygonal ornamental boulders, live oaks with hanging epiphytes, all of it reduced to fit in a one-bedroom apartment, a table, a kitchen island with stools, a pretty backsplash of ceramic tiles from her native Guadalajara.

Her eyes are not close together but they seem circular and in front of her head. Her light accent, the way she always said *Francisco* with more music than anyone else, her general friendliness, made me like her right away when we met long ago, plus I think she liked that I spoke Spanish, not that I ever spoke much with her. The mothers of long-time friends, there's something there, a mutual observation society. We've known each other for so many years, have seen each other age, can track our own age in the other, and there's of course shared intimate yet very different knowledge of son and friend. We both see *Francisco* not as a man approaching fifty but in part at eighteen, rangy, now stabilized, solidified, still trying to figure things out, apt to over-analyze, waft analysis about relationships and expectations of masculinity et cetera into the air in such a way that it never comes down. Overall, maybe because he's trim and dresses well enough and often smiles, like the Joker, he gets the benefit of the doubt.

I had called him earlier in the year, in April, same week the Notre Dame cathedral burned, when everything was going down with my father and the move from Philadelphia. Wireless headphones on, sitting on a bench at lunch in Washington Square near the colonial buildings in Old City, but he couldn't talk, at work, suggested he also had big news he'd share at some point. I assumed he was moving to New Zealand where his wife was from, the other side of the world, what an existence, an unexpected shift in the geographical experience. Texas to Ohio to Chicago to Marfa to Brooklyn to New Zealand. Your geographical career like a professional athlete's tour from team to team, unexpectedly traded to Auckland or Wellington, the way I was unexpectedly traded from South Philadelphia to the Rose Valley/Media/Swarthmore suburb. After a time we lose our freewill when it's combined with the needs of our families, flexible, able to adapt, no longer dependent on geography to establish identity, able to live anywhere and be who we are, and if it's not a good fit at first we know after a while we'll evolve and find what we need in the new location.

Kiko's mother in this relatively new location, although she's been in Brooklyn for seven or eight years now, at least by the time Kiko's daughter was born five years ago.

Renata's hiding under a table, tall and thin, hair trimmed straight framing her face. She's very much unlike my daughter, I say, who is the opposite of shy, who runs up and hugs random people on the street, no concept of stranger danger.

I'm offered food I politely decline. I do need to charge my phone, however, so we sit and talk for fifteen minutes, all while Renny goes to the bedroom and returns wearing a different outfit, parades around, makes a goofy face, and then returns to the bedroom. She does this over and over, displaying a princess getup, a mermaid outfit (Halloween costume), a green turtleneck incompletely pulled over her head as she shuffles in grunting and groaning like some deformed monster.

I say I don't get to see many other kids since we've moved. I really only see Kali and the few kids who live nearby. In the city I saw hundreds every day at the playground, on the street, when I dropped Kali at school I saw how she was different. Kali would never hide under a table and then put on a fashion show, would never seek attention, if she ever put down her tablet she would invade your personal space, lean on you, ask a question about invasive species like English ivy or stinkbugs or tell a joke that doesn't make sense like what do you call a stinkbug atop another stinkbug? A stinkbug sandwich. That sort of thing.

Why does she joke about stinkbugs?

We have stinkbugs, alas. She traps them and keeps them as pets. Otherwise there's little we can do but swat them. They smell like cilantro when smushed.

No stinkbugs here, Kiko's mother says, no bedbugs either I hope.

She asks why I'm in town.

To see a band at the Garden, I say.

She asks which band and what kind of music they play.

They're difficult to categorize, I say. Adventuresome, playful, ornate songs, huge jams. In 2017 they played Madison Square Garden on thirteen consecutive nights and didn't repeat a song, playing 274 songs total.

Kiko's mother frowns and says she's never heard of them.

I say they're never on the radio or anything like that.

She says I'm welcome to stay here instead of returning to Philadelphia.

I thank her but who knows what state I'll be in and by the time I'd make it back here from the Garden I could be halfway to my mother's place in New Jersey.

She asks about my father. I tell her how when we visited the nursing home yesterday he seemed nearly as bad physically as mentally. I don't mention swollen ankles and gnarly toenails, how scabs and scars from decades of solar overexposure have transformed his chest into a topographical map of Mars. I don't mention the elderly pale woman, so ethereal she seemed nearly erased, one hand steadying herself against the wall of a long hallway, saying over and over *I can't breathe.* I don't tell her how after the nursing home I introduced Mamou and Kali to the Rhombus at the Institute for Advanced Study before getting take-out wings at Chuck's.

We talk about the election, the Democratic candidates. She says it seems like Bernie has the most support in New York. I say I'm not sure about Pennsylvania, we'll see. I mention how I paid too much attention once the new administration took power. I wanted to end it all for everyone but since of course I wouldn't be able to do that it was frustrating but I'm surprised that someone with nothing to live for, with a good working knowledge of firearms and spare time to spend at the shooting range, hasn't taken him out. Or of course he could be poisoned. And then I say whenever I talk like this or even think it I assume an app on my phone notifies the CIA and agents deploy.

I don't tell her how at the free show at The Met in Philadelphia, December 3, 2019, I knew it was induced but I was also pretty sure that some people around me were federal agents watching me on account of the opening pages of *Neutral Evil)))* about wanting to put on the suit I wore to our wedding, get a sweet fascist haircut, and then take the train to DC, tap politely on the window of the Oval Office, be invited in, and do the deed. It seemed inevitable that someone would do it but it hadn't happened maybe because I was destined to do it? It would never happen unless I made it happen. That particular door was only open for me to walk through.

Thoughts like these expressed in a short novel, ostensibly fiction but clearly the type of fiction that isn't invented, made me think the young guy with the goatee from New Jersey, a music therapist who said he works with kids with autism like Kali and adults with Alzheimer's like my father, was really an agent scoping me out. Maybe phans seemed straighter than they did when I saw them in the early '90s or maybe it had something to do with too many edibles and too many hits off passed vape pens, paranoid albeit aware of course that the feds probably wouldn't bother to scope me out, engage me, discern the degree to which I was a threat, and neutralize me in the middle of a concert attended by two thousand people, although it would be a good time to do so since I wouldn't be expecting governmental engagement in those circumstances, plus I was susceptible to free and incriminating speech, even if people I talked to at the show only talked about the band, shows they'd seen, songs they wanted to hear. I nevertheless couldn't stop thinking that some in my vicinity were government agents.

Kiko's mother says they probably don't have enough agents to investigate everyone who's said such a thing in the vicinity of their phones.

Mine is all charged so we get ready to go. Ren begs her daddy not to leave, puts up a fuss. Near the door there's an old family photograph I didn't see when entering the apartment but now remember seeing at Kiko's house in Houston in early 1992. It's from the '80s, Kiko's father was alive, the kids are kids, the mom looks the same, tanner. She invites me to stay with them whenever I'm in town, we hug, and then Kiko and I are on the sidewalk, stretching our legs, out in the open air, the unconstrained city.

He says he's thankful for his mother and sister and his sister's legally married female partner but I can tell he needs an outing, a long walk with an old male friend, he needs to move and talk and see things and tire himself out, get out of his head.

The street toward Prospect Park is tree-lined, individual houses, almost Midwestern, with porches. I say something about trees that grow in Brooklyn. We talk about dad jokes and the dad bod, although Kiko, like Mamou, had always been effortlessly trim. Kiko's wife, the Kiwi curator, had gained weight after the pregnancy. I saw her in their Red Hook apartment not long after Renata's birth. She wore a loose-fitting dress like a hospital gown, floral, formless. But then recently she regained her former shape as she transitioned from fine-art curating to waiting tables and now managing a high-end Indonesian restaurant in TriBeCa, no longer strictly vegan.

She'd had anxiety issues most likely exacerbated by the blow to her ego when it became clear she wouldn't continue as a curator in New York after her initial temporary position at the prestigious midtown museum ended, which had gone well enough but it didn't help that she was from New Zealand, also that she was now the mother of a young girl, getting older, not doing what she'd studied. So once she recovered her form, she rebelled, going out for drinks after the Indonesian restaurant closed, coming home late, one time not coming home at all. She'd been sleeping with a waiter at the Indonesian restaurant. Kiko called with all this information in October, although it had come to light in April, same time as everything with my dad and the move.

A motorcycle blasts down a prototypical Brooklyn street as we cross it, causing us to accelerate toward Prospect Park. Kiko talks about his situation. I'm actively trying to listen, but I can't stop interjecting, trying to sway thoughts toward optimism, even as I tell myself *just listen, let him talk*, like some sort of meditative practice. Clear all thoughts other than the voice of your friend.

His wife plans to move out soon after New Year's. The logistics of it all, the furniture she took, the appliances, chairs, there's nowhere to sit in the apartment now. He asks if I want to see it, a few blocks that way. He points toward some sandy bright building glowing in the distance, but I'd prefer to keep moving, get him in the park, a walk in the park this man needs.

His thoughts are broken, his concentration dispersed in mother's apartment where daughter will spend afternoon and formerly shared apartment now half empty where so much recent drama went down, subjecting one another to some real abuse, verbal and psychic, as though the force, the volume and intensity of words expelled by the wholly human emotions of anger and despair and betrayal were worse on the moral balance sheet than the precipitating actions, those that caused him to lose his cool, the foundation of fidelity and trust and honesty and everything considered good and required for a relationship undermined by her action, even if it was a reaction to something he did or didn't do or continuously did without necessarily doing anything intentional, just *his being*, the emanation of his spirit, his scent and stench, daily exposure to unprotected intimate humanity, back and forth, every day, living in the city with a kid and not a lot of money, the mother no longer pursuing what she spent years studying, the temporal and financial expense of that pursuit not wasted but not in play as expected.

Of all the scenarios when they moved to New York so she could get her curatorial degree, the one in which she's managing a restaurant a few years later and moving out after an affair with a waiter only compares favorably to mortal tragedy. Better than dying in a freak accident or contracting a terrible illness, the current disruption's instability and total uncertainty, can't imagine at this stage figuring out how to live without wife and child every day— man, I'm sorry, there's definitely no way to consider it ideal, although I suppose you now get to experience the opening stages of love again without guilt or at least fulfill lust with someone new for the first time. There's that, the inevitability of renewal, even if it's sad awkward inebriated divorcée-on-divorcé action, momentum toward that first post-marital conquest, it's something to look forward to, a consolation prize—you're a handsome man, *fundamentally good* without being angelic or a Christian soldier devoted to charity or even volunteering much, you're all over the place in your own quiet way, sure, permanently in something of a meditative frazzled semi-morose state, and apt to laugh about it, I'll grant you that, but I also guarantee that what's left of your life won't be spent in a state of involuntary celibacy.

He says that's *not true*, he does good deeds now and then. He recently helped his sister on one of her projects— and there she is, playing soccer on an encaged AstroTurf field. She's playing center fullback, wearing all black, must be fifty years old but from a distance seems no older than she did twenty-five years ago when at the Harvard Divinity School at the same time I lived across town in Jamaica Plain. Kiko often visited Boston from Chicago for extended stays with both of us, a few months after his father had died. We listened to the second Nas record at his sister's apartment, disappointed it wasn't as good as *Illmatic*. Kiko wanted to talk about his father's death. I may not have been the most generous or understanding or patient friend at the time, a gorgeous spring afternoon in Cambridge, situationally depressed, just beginning to arrange my escape from crappy cold weather and oil heating costs exceeding monthly rent, making $7/hour at an antiquarian bookstore, wrapping and shipping rare books to send to customers around the world who'd ordered over the Internet (capitalized at the time like that), which I hadn't yet "surfed." Oh how I needed Netflix and dating apps, spending too much on movie rentals, the manager of the video store guilting me into walking her home from the bar and then trying to get me to kiss her, a change of scenery was needed, so I moved back to my parents' house in New Jersey, and wound up writing my first book (about living at my parents' house and temping to save enough to travel by land to Peru).

His sister waves after he yells her name. He asks if I want to stop and talk.

I say let's keep moving, seems like she's in the middle of something here.

He says it's a noncompetitive game, she's run it for like fifteen years.

I say how can you play noncompetitively?

He says they're just getting some exercise, treating it like a game without getting *aggressive* about winning or anything.

In an affected scientific white guy voice I say if I'm truthful with you, based on your explanation and my observation of the activity at hand, I'm sorry but your sister's noncompetitive soccer playtime here seems like *a game for losers,* and then I stagger and slap my knee with tongue out, and then apologize for doing a bad Chappelle imitation, the problem of course being that what I said wasn't funny.

I ask, more seriously, if he's played in this noncompetitive soccer game?

He says yeah but he's too good for it, it's hard to ensure everyone's having fun.

Compassionate, empathetic sports, I say. Compassionate, empathetic war.

Bomb them softly, he says, feel their pain.

We've reached the outer ring of the park, exposed to varieties of unorganized individual athletic experience. Bikers, walkers. No angry mob of joggers. Rollerblading seems less popular—we'll call that progress. I very much expect we'll see someone from college. Almost no way we won't.

Oh I feel like they filmed a "High Maintenance" scene around here, along the water. But we don't talk about the show, how after every episode I say to Mamou "best thing on TV," the closest to short stories, natural constructions based of theme and association without seeming intentionally naturalistic, artful cinematography without seeming artsy, actors not seeming like they're acting, TV unlike TV.

In an alternate reality I'm familiar with every undulation in the path we walk and the road around it. When I lived in Greenpoint, I'd run around the crappy soccer field in McCarren Park, turning my head from dust vortices, always with a taste of straight-up dirt in my mouth, so it's possible I would have found my way to Prospect Park, especially if I moved to Clinton Hill or Fort Greene. So many variables, no way of knowing. Could've gone in the other direction, smoking, drinking, harder drugs, Long Island City, Queens. Lord knows. I suppose if I hadn't met Mamou in Philadelphia nine years ago and instead transferred to the New York office when offered an opportunity there it's likely I would have found myself running around this park, another Olmstead production like Central Park, same as my high school's campus, same as FDR park in South Philly near the stadiums, same as around Jamaica Pond near where I'd lived in Boston, these hundred-year-old Olmstead parks, the undulating paved path not too wide or narrow, the water element, trees at regular intervals, the black-stemmed lamps.

We talk about certainty, uncertainty, family versus self, marriage, fidelity, options, the future. What weighs on him, as though his thoughts emanate a leaden cloud, is uncertainty. He needs to identify concerns, know what they are, list them, prioritize them, and then write down what he needs from wife and family. He needs bulleted lists, clear efficient emotionless language transmitted to wife delineating what's required to reestablish stability as soon as possible during this period of transition. He's been churning on it, professing feelings like a champ, but he needs to get everything in order. He wants everything to be fifty fifty, so he should present what he wants, how things should be divided, in writing, via email, without emotion or regret, total focus on certainty for all.

Marriage is certainty, knowing *if* you're going to marry (yes!) and *who* and *when* you're going to marry (spouse on wedding day!), two uncertainties that weigh on so many through their twenties and thirties. Having a child brings even more certainty, restrictions attendant to parental responsibility ultimately beneficial because they maximize certainty. There's no question what you have to do. Can't move to Alaska on a whim. He's lucky that his primary responsibility is his daughter. His decisions need to be about her. But you can lose yourself in family, in privileging parental responsibilities over other needs, everything that had previously been who you were and what you did, without which, what are you? Who are you? Lose it too much and your wife doesn't respect you. Maybe she tries to regain her own sense of independence, of who she is, favoring the excitement of uncertainty over the same-old certainty the family brings.

She achieved certainty by creating chaos, exploding familial certainty, neglecting responsibility, blaming him for pushing her away with moody critical behavior, how he yelled at everyone on Thanksgiving the previous year, the specifics not retold with much clarity but involving everyone (all women: mother, wife, sister, sister's partner) critiquing his behavior, coaching him how to parent, saying he's *doing it wrong*, could do it better. Sister and wife not besties, some friction there always, always the sense he and wife could take daughter to New Zealand for good, abandoning aunt and grandmother after considerable investment of time and care. No one knows the future, so there's anticipatory anxiety about unknown future events.

We can see Park Slope apartments on the other side of a wavy open field, not quite hilly enough for sledding, if it ever snows again. We have a direction now, shooting for an exit blocks from Grand Army Plaza.

Constant machete work through the vines of time. New York feels like an old skill, neurological pathways clogged with the past, the walk along Seventh Avenue in Park Slope, the subway stop where there used to be a movie theater on Flatbush. When I first visited a friend who lived nearby more than twenty years ago the street flowed with young Black dudes in puffy coats. We get on the subway there, surrounded by young white women wearing weird cigarette-like fragments of plastic in their ears. I smelled poo on the platform and now on the train and am worried I stepped in something or sat in something or am just unclean although I showered in the morning and am wearing fresh clothes. There's a stench in my nostrils, not too strong but insistent, maybe on the platform someone had pooped? There's a nearby baby carriage occupied by an infant but it doesn't quite smell like baby poo. Maybe it's just something in the air.

Saturday afternoon, Lower East Side under a clear sky, looking for a bar Kiko knows. He plans to see an Adam Sandler movie once I go to the show. I consider getting him a ticket, invite him to come hide in the herd, but it's expensive, and last time I took him to a show of this sort he wasn't into it. The first Dead show (September 7, 1990) after Brent's death, at the Richfield Coliseum outside Cleveland. So difficult to achieve a semblance of symbiosis with a friend seated next to me not seeming into it. We were in the upper deck, center, far from the stage, tickets a tenth of what tonight's show cost. Buying a ticket for Kiko tonight and achieving immersion in timelessness and joy, pretty sure he wouldn't float with the flock, wouldn't enjoy semi-requisite psychoactive supplementary activities, although there's always a chance the band does something stupendous, the crowd jubilates, and exposure to unleashed nondenominational positivity infects him with something approaching religious fervor thanks to disappearance en masse into time suspended by music and lights.

I'm sure if ecstatic communal experience were available tonight he'd be into it but the feeling isn't guaranteed. No chance the show won't be good. At worst it'll be lackluster, sans surprises. Some say their *off nights* are better than most bands' *best nights*. But even a great night might be lost on him in his current state, also he's never been a fan of improvisation, not even jazz, always liked tighter bands, precision, percussion. Goofier aspects of the band, humor, silliness, turns off anyone with a punk bone in their body, although he saw them in the early '90s too, so some time travel may be available.

He returned from the Agora Theater in Cleveland one night after seeing Nirvana around the time "Nevermind" came out, everyone infected exactly as though they'd seen something that someone who hadn't gone to the show would write about almost thirty years later. Dopey looks on their faces as though in the best possible way they'd all been royally fucked, sober more or less, inspired, wanting to replicate it, duplicate it, recreate it somehow.

I don't remember Kiko seeing the band the first time I saw them at the campus bar, called the 'Sco, short for *disco*. I missed the first song, pregaming, smoking, drinking a little maybe, but once there I plugged into my spot on the floor, energized, mesmerized, hypnotized. The drummer a hairy little ogre in goggles and donut-patterned dress; the bass player as stoic as John Entwistle or Bill Wyman with a mop of hair obscuring his face except for a spectacular nose; the keyboardist a clean-cut choir boy in white button-down; the guitarist with thick red hair, boxy metal-framed

glasses, white leather high-tops with the tongues out, leaning in and out so the middle part in his hair created a fear-
some symmetry as he introduced a theme and added to it
and pushed it and transformed it all into a chainsaw that
ripped ahead and mega-evolved into something pure and
soaring and saturated with joy, sound that if squeezed from
the corners of your eyes and tested would reveal pure sero-
tonin.

I later learned that the band's primary writer, singer,
and guitarist grew up in Princeton and even played for our
township's hockey team (Lawrence) on the Prep School's
rink around the time my father and I used to walk our
collie there and stop to warm up and watch on Saturday
mornings. Crazy to think we may have seen him on the
ice as a teenager. He also was among the first employees
at the Princeton Record Exchange, and it's crazy to think I
may have bought my first record ("Dark Side of the Moon")
from him.

All grown up now leading this band, from Vermont apparently, they seemed dangerous, like they could do anything. They filled the room with dry-ice smoke, cranked a
strobe light, and jumped on trampolines in time, and then
the drummer sang a Syd Barrett song and took a solo by
holding a vacuum cleaner nozzle to his mouth and the mic,
gimmicks easing extreme virtuosic excellence.

From April 1991 through their 1993/'94 New Year's
show at the Worcester Centrum, I saw them fifteen times,
at small venues, like the Capital Theater in Port Chester,
NY—the day after Thanksgiving 1992 the best by far, fourth

row in front of the bass player, well spun. It would've been Jimi Hendrix's fiftieth birthday (hard to believe I'm now nearly as old as Jimi would've been that day). It was like discovering some new technology, tracking something special and unknown yet monumental that would spread. They were so original and dynamic and *weird* yet also good-natured there was no way their audience wouldn't grow because everyone who saw them came away shocked and persuaded, effusive, evangelical spirits ignited.

It was something to look forward to, something to do, a party, fun, always refreshing, at times transcendent, but then there was that New Year's show '93/'94. No longer at the campus disco for seven bucks or a small theater, this was an arena. The three sets they played that night and aquarium gag at midnight may now be considered among their greatest, but not for me in the upper deck, off to the bass player's side, too much to drink and smoke, the kids around me younger and on acid and not doing well. Had I grown out of it already, just twenty one? That show at the Worcester Centrum, upper deck in a goddamn arena, plus the song "If I Could" on the band's latest album, combined to undermine my love. That song, after two straightforward rockers, seemed like an affront. Its existence almost evoked tears. How could the same band that wrote quasi-classical cartoonish epics resolving in soaring jams, how could the same humans write "If I Could"?! They were selling out arenas writing shit like "If I Could"?

Senior year in college I heard Can's "Tago Mago" and "Ege Bamyasi" for the first time, Gastr del Sol's "The Serpentine Similar," Fela's "Black Man's Cry" and "Original Sufferhead," The Meters' "Look A-Py-Py," saw Polvo at the 'Sco for five bucks, started listening to old country blues, classic post-bop, Mingus particularly, Coltrane's "Africa/Brass," Andrew Hill, Sam Rivers, Sun Ra. "If I Could" was not only affront and betrayal, it was launchpad into everything else, each part of a smaller movement, not its own thing like the Dead, its own self-enclosed genre essentially, each now with their own satellite radio station streaming crystalline recordings of live concerts some of which I went to when I was seventeen, eighteen, glancing at the dashboard display and announcing to Kali behind me "I was there" as the Dead station plays a song from the Shoreline Amphitheater shows, mid-June 1990, or JFK Stadium in Philly, July 7, 1989.

But at the time, without question, it was over for me after that '93/'94 New Year's arena show. I didn't see them again until a few days after Thanksgiving 2003, nearly ten years, didn't listen to them, knew none of their new albums or songs. I went with hometown friends, the extraordinary power of the first few songs, old favorites, but then ten new songs in a row, straightforward compared to what I'd loved, each with twenty minutes of explorative soaring as dudes in fleece jackets played air guitar all around, normal-looking guys jerking shoulders and bending knees possibly out of their minds on psychedelics, which fit with the relatively tame, conventional, straightforward song structures that took off on epic improvisational excursions, interesting at times but automatic, like the band was going through the motions.

Reviews online for that show call it one of their worst ever. One guy said he was tearing up during it. Everyone qualifying they're not trolls and love the band but this was their least favorite of dozens they'd seen up to that point and afterwards. And this was the first show I'd seen in a decade. It therefore didn't occur to me to see them again until I was offered a free ticket for a summer midweek show at the Mann Music Center, August 12, 2015, an amphitheater easy enough to get to from South Philly.

It was a warm Wednesday or Thursday night. Before the show, Crow handed me half a goo ball and then smiling like some cracked trickster physician, his light-blue eyes their usual squinty red behind mirrored aerodynamic prescription skier sunglasses, he offered me a pill and a vape pen. Inside the venue, immediately separated from friends who had lower level tickets and planned to sneak me down, I found the seat specified on my ticket, on the concrete area between the covered half-dome and the lawn. I talked with neighbors, said I hadn't seen the band since 1993, completely forgetting the 2003 show. Neighbors said I was in for a treat, they've been playing great, lots of good new stuff, playing the old stuff accurately. They started with an old rocker and my neighbors slapped me on the shoulder like here's one for ya ol' timer, and passed me a vape pen and then another old one and then songs I didn't recognize that sounded great, turning from the stage toward the crowd on the lawn behind me as the sun set, everyone flushed, vibrant, joyous. The pill kicking in must have been Adderall. I had complete control of movement, anticipating every rhythmic variation, music and movement in sync, especially with old-favorite composed pieces.

Anonymity, encroaching darkness, and crowd density and focus on stage and screens created an unselfconscious space to operate. My head kept time, back and forth. Vestibular oscillation made every sound seem processed through an enormous Leslie speaker. The kick-drum influenced my heartbeat. Every song seemed inspired, connection between band and crowd symbiotic. And thanks to the pill I'd been given I was *very focused* on the sound, thoughts clear, coherent, concocting future writing projects, essayistic, experiential, aerodynamic, everything in it without seeming maximalist, thoughts I didn't thumb to my phone as they occurred to conserve their semblance and so lost it all other than a sliver of a sense of it. Crow found me at intermission and stood beside me during the second set as they played five songs total, each lasting twenty minutes or more, having no idea which song or even *which set* it was, completely out of time, hanging on every note. It took a while (twenty-two years) but I was back on the train.

The next morning I downloaded the mp3s via a code on my ticket and listened multiple times, enjoying it, glad it held up, and eventually the monster jams of the second set seemed composed. Improvisation transformed into brilliant organic patient group composition. So good.

Every morning after they played a show I received an email with the set list, always wondering if I would have liked it, did they play old songs I knew or new ones, but I had no real inclination to see them again until I bought a ticket to go solo to Camden in late June 2019, bought it well before we started looking at houses or moved.

No one I knew would be around, I'd just go same way I see any band in the city, head out solo, eat some edibles, immerse myself in the music, leaning on the stage in front of Espers and Vetiver and Ryley Walker, or right up front for Dylan Carlson, Chris Forsyth, Endless Boogie, 75 Dollar Bill, Tortoise, Destroyer, never disappointed, never spending more than $15 or so on a ticket, walking or taking the train to the venue, at most three beers, but seeing the band outside at Camden wouldn't be so bad.

An old friend from the Princeton area scored a ticket a week before the show. It hadn't sold out. We met in the lot and wandered around and drank seventeen-dollar beers on a perfect night, ate edibles and hit everything passed our way. The show was a Saturday Night Special, high energy, big hits, new favorites, jams of course but more focused on rocking the house, and then we wandered around the parking lot and made it back before too late. In the morning I cleaned and cleaned (John Martyn's album "Solid Air" on repeat sounding so good, still kinda stoned) and handed off the keys to the tenants, laughing at the chorus of "Bertha" ("I had to move, -oove, really had to moo-hoo-oove") on the radio when I started the car to take the last load of crap to the new house and complete our move.

Just like that we're wandering the Lower East Side looking for a bar Kiko knows, down here, over there, somewhere nearby? It's closed, won't open for an hour, so we peek into a Mexican restaurant, one table occupied by a family, kids wearing headphones immersed in tablets.

That's my life right there, I say, eating out between lunch and dinner so we don't distract otherwise unoccupied adults.

It's loud and warm, the tables seem rickety, haphazard, there's something unwelcoming about it, smells of bleach, so we cross the street to a more inviting, empty Mexican place and order tacos and beer.

Kiko sits beneath a long window looking out on the street. He man-spreads and drapes arms over adjoining chairs and says that was a good walk. We talk about how walking synchronizes everything, chills you out, tires you so you can sleep so the next day you have more energy. I show him the pedometer on my phone, the one-year graph. It's fallen off each month after our move from 15K to 7K/day, corresponding with more drinking, eating whatever, clothes tighter, anxiety elevating, restlessness, all obviously attributed to increased consumption of carbohydrates, sugar, and alcohol mixed with decreased movement.

The tacos are nearly twice the price as those in South Philly yet nowhere near twice as good. Still, combined with the beer, they're delicious, restorative, *and so it begins* I say, talking about how this is my vacation, my *grand solo indulgence*, although I'm a little concerned I'll be worn down by the walk across Prospect Park, all over the Lower East Side, and then after tacos up through the East Village, over to a basement bar I like, the sun already down behind the buildings.

Scratcher is dark and warm, as always, not too loud. Nineteen years ago, that table over there, the writer from London, head on my shoulder, reciting Shakespeare. Seventeen years ago with the writer from Iowa, at the bar. Another time I sat in the same seat extinguishing nerves with hefeweizen before a reading at a nearby venue (Fez, closed long ago) as I folded printouts of my stories into paper airplanes I'd throw to the crowd as I read about how I wasn't going to read that night.

Kiko, midway through a single Guinness, reveals that his estranged wife is related to the last woman New Zealand put to death for murdering her husband.

At least she didn't cut you into little pieces, I say. There's *that*.

He talks about going on meds, about mixed identity.

We talk about not belonging to a group.

I talk about the band, togetherness, timelessness.

I eat an Adderall that Crow gave me last time he was back east after moving to the Lake Tahoe area. I have three beers to Kiko's one.

All too fluently I talk about how Kali says I'm going to get synesthesia like it's a readily available sensation, how the complicated composed songs at this point in their career indicate the degree to which they're on top of their shit, if executed with precision and presence, not a recital but four musicians and the light guy united with twenty thousand dancing to music that shouldn't be danceable, bodies attuned to every point and counterpoint, which brings everyone together, these complicated sections, the peculiar particularity that made us fall for their music in the first place, that caught ears and made us play it for others, how I brought home a compact disc of their second album (released in 1990 on an independent label, Absolute A Go Go Records) and two or three live cassettes after my first year in college and shared them with everyone, selecting the one with the catchy chorus to play first, the one Kali sings whenever it comes on their dedicated Sirius radio station now, the catchy one with the intricate part followed by the two-chord soaring major key jam.

Seconds later we're out where the Bowery bleeds into Cooper Union and Third Avenue around East Sixth Street. The restaurant at the southeastern corner seemed to change every few years twenty years ago but now seems settled as a woody craft-beer gastropub. We hug it out and Kiko heads south toward Houston to see that Adam Sandler movie alone before returning to the demons in his cave. I move west toward Broadway, eat a gummy, cut through Washington Square. Fewer trees. Full-on night now. I photograph the Christmas tree with the Empire State Building in the distance through the arch, post it with the caption "the ghosts of Christmas past saying want sense, want sense," referencing first impressions of Washington Square, roving men selling sinsemilla, weed without seed, put out of business by delivery services and mounted

police presence. By the time I get to the Sixth Avenue subway I delete it, maybe because I don't want to announce I'm
in New York and don't want to post blurry images from the
show for no one's delight and then have a dead battery on
the way back. My phone needs to survive since my train
ticket home is on the New Jersey Transit app.

Thumbing this to my phone on the train to work,
March 13, 2020, it's pouring and the train seems empty
thanks to the coronavirus interrupting all activities, sports
seasons suspended, stock market crashed, supermarkets
stripped as everyone prepares for life without regular dis-
tributions and processes, my employer not yet letting me
work from home, still in *code yellow*. Not until my child's
school closes will I be allowed to work from home daily,
which seems imminent, the obvious next step.

I interrupt the otherwise linear progression about December 28, 2019 in part because I can't really remember if
I took the train to Penn Station or walked up Seventh or
Eighth Avenue to Madison Square Garden, stopping first
for another pre-game beer at the Blarney Stone, a not particularly classy bar I sometimes sit at while waiting for a
train back to Philly, but now it's a different vibe. Big dude
in the doorway lets me in and it's packed with Westchester
County and Long Island phans, burly guys of Italian and
Jewish descent in shirts purchased at previous shows at the
Garden, like Islanders fans ready to rock out to intricate
playful epics written in the mid-'80s.

I slide in at the bar, get a beer, and talk to a guy
seated there. He looks like a high school cross-country run-

ner, a scholar/athlete, wearing an official T-shirt from the donut shows at the Garden in summer 2017 when they played thirteen consecutive nights, each with its own donut theme (complimentary donuts distributed courtesy of Federal Donuts, located a few blocks east of our place in South Philly), and didn't repeat a song. Amtrak was under construction so I heard it was a hassle to get there from New Jersey and Philadelphia, but that's all forgotten a couple years later, everyone having listened to those shows, especially the *jelly donut* show where they *jammed* every song at unexpected times, extending for example a short song about synesthesia to thirty minutes, a video of which I once played for Kali, talking about smelling the colors, "overwhelmed by olfactory hues," something she returned to as she does days and weeks later whenever I mention the band or play them, especially in October and November as I listened for the first time to their "new" albums (all those that came out after 1993), streaming them from phone to a cranked portable speaker as I grilled and drank good beer, with Kali sitting on the back deck with her tablet, backdropped by neverending autumnal splendor.

"Punch You in the Eye" comes on the jukebox and I share my excitement about hearing it at a bar. I don't think I've ever heard them at a bar, let alone "Punch You in the Eye." The guy I'm talking to says he put it on, put his money in forty-five minutes ago. Crazy that out of everyone in the bar you're the guy who put it on, I say. He'd only started seeing them fifteen years ago, has seen them fifty-something times, mostly at the Garden. I relay my story, which impresses him since he didn't exist in 1991. It's like someone telling me about seeing The Dead in the late '60s before I was born.

I feel a surge toward the show a few blocks away, the drink and edibles and Adderall coming together, having only eaten two tacos. I need to steady myself, need to approach with some caution, get inside the venue, find my seat. Most of my concert-going experience in small clubs and bars. Arena Rock Concert Experience I've really only enjoyed a few times, Jerry Garcia Band shows in 1989 and 1992. Yes in 1987 or so. Pink Floyd with my mom and friends at the Brendan Byrne Arena a little before that. The Dead at The Spectrum in 1988 and Richfield Coliseum in 1990, 1991, and 1993 but otherwise always saw them outside.

Security check, metal detector, airport-ish, too bright, nasty concessions, the same circular concourse transposed, Knicks and Rangers advertisements and memorabilia instead of Sixers and Flyers. Got a beer somehow, however much it costs. Found my seat, coats saving seats nearby, can't imagine abandoning my coat on one of these nineteen thousand seats. Adderall working, gummy working, tired from walking, walked way too much, drank too much on a nearly empty stomach, fuddled, groggy, should've taken it easy. Similar vantage to the ill-fated New Year's show, '93/'94 Worcester Centrum, upper deck, bass player's side. Sense that what's around you is unique and important yet there it is again and again and again, replicated in strange yet similar ways every ten feet in all directions, clusters having unique important experiences compounded. No jumbotron. Summer amphitheater shows benefit from large screens fracturing the visual field.

The inside skin of the Garden looks like the Death Star, cavernous, striated, sandy, inner membrane of a shell the music will crack open to reveal a sea of stars we touch with fingertips, ruby waves pouring down on our heads, something along those lines maybe. I didn't necessarily anticipate being this intoxicated in such an expansive indoor environment.

I sit, I'll sit here, wait for the band to come on, the seat next to me occupied by a young guy who I sense grew up Hasidic. His facial hair is sparse and his skin smooth, like he's never shaved and his beard won't thicken until his life gets harder. He's been to about thirty shows, mostly at the Garden, in the past ten years. He's probably in his late twenties.

I've entered full-on godawful flowing philosophical mode, able to trace in speech undefined and really actually usually invisible thoughts, focused on the band at this point of course, a variety of what I said to Kiko about the composed complicated parts as a test that brings everyone together, a recitation, an invocation, a virtuosity gauntlet, extreme complexity, the sort of thing that makes Yes or Rush seem straightforward, the music altogether locked in time, without room for anything other than flubs, only occasionally do they improvise around the known core of the composition, half-assing it for novelty or not being up to the challenge, how they envy Keith Richards pleasing crowds with the "Satisfaction" riff whereas to achieve a similar response they need to play their most complicated old songs and do so perfectly, aware how hard it will be in their seventies, in twenty years, assuming survival. So these recitations/invocations are endangered, perishable, the way it's no longer possible to see the JGB led by Garcia himself.

The presumably lapsed Hasidic kid and I sit close like on a bargain airline. I'm profusely verbose and apologetic about such perfusion, apologetic in part for not being able to effortlessly return to the point of departure, tangents taking over, my talk fluidly fragmentary, good-natured controlled chaos, talking about how the ability to follow digressive shit-talking paths back to the starting point is the hallmark of sanity, shit-togetherness, but once you no longer remember where you started, watch out. My father in the nursing home the previous day, December 27, 2019, unable to recognize the pants my mother had purchased for him, new shoes, thinking he was in someone else's room.

I ask the guy next to me if his parents are devoutly religious, he nods and, before he can elaborate, the show starts. Huge roar, little familiar forms on stage, a new song, its debut, about approaching the night with caution, an energy-sucking downer for a Saturday night opener, like late-era Dead songs I first heard at concerts that seemed like a new product line no one really wanted, although these guys are endlessly creative, always writing, they challenge themselves to write something technically easy yet solid and subtle, moving, yet no one really comes for that.

The second song they play was new when I stopped listening to them in the early '90s, not interested in straight-ahead rock, although now it's a classic from nearly thirty years ago. The current version enters so-called "type 2" improvisation. It breaks from the song structure and extends and stretches and morphs, an elastic epic concocted on the spot.

No idea what song the jam emerged from at one point, couldn't remember until they returned to the original song structure. I'm laughing since they clearly wiped my memory, as though the improvisational section erased the traditional song structure, the unconventional vanquished the conventional, the ecstatic overcame the commercial, timelessness trumped temporal, but even typing "trumped" is too loaded, undermines this sentence's multi-car pile-up of phrases, although there's no sense he's the president during the show. It's a non-political space, dedicated to something else, something *more*, and of course it's a political space since everything is political from the perspective of those obsessed with politics so if it's apolitical it's political in tacit consent to authoritarianism and idiocy et cetera ad infinitum, an equation that doesn't seem to consider that a non-political space can be utopian, idealistic, open, inclusive, joyful, all of which can convey to civic life, to the vote, plus there's a sense that most fans are Bernie types, the band associated with Sanders from Burlington as well as liberal charities but they're not an overtly political band, the way the Dead believed being explicitly "anti-war" was still about war and they wanted to create an alternative space, same way the band expresses extreme aesthetic independence, does so to an extent I'm sure loses fans as they veer into territories deemed goofy, corny, sentimental, indulgent, totally uncool.

Laughable distracting worrisome paranoia returns that unaccompanied young men on either side have been assigned to assess the degree to which I might follow through on declarations regarding a strong yet unactionable desire to assassinate Trump. Recurrence of such a mental state relates, at best, to inherited trauma imprinted and passed down along the paternal Eastern European Ashkenazi side of my lineage. At work I sometimes feel low-level irrational persecution anxiety, as does another Jewish colleague, and I sometimes wonder if it explains why we're such productive workers, as though centuries of persecution compel us to please corporate superiors by surpassing expectations. Vague delusional paranoia can be a positive protective factor in a wholly innocuous work environment. But stirred free range in a crowd during a time of rising intolerance and authoritarianism, spurred by intake on a nearly empty stomach of various perception disruptors, maybe it's not so valuable?

Guy to my left is a good deal shorter, scraggly blond beard, twenty-something, willing to smoke the joint I smuggled into the venue in a little plastic tube in my underwear after hearing about intense Garden security. Spliff mixed with fine tobacco burns slowly, a housewarming gift from a college friend (*muchas gracias*, San!) who sent lawfully procured goods from an enlightened western state including this joint I saved for months that burns beautifully after I light it as the jam for "Twenty Years Later" starts. The potential federal agent to my left with the scraggly beard passes it back and forth several times but the potentially formerly Hasidic guy on my right declines. I realize of course that paranoia is induced, an unintentional expression of concern about this temporary reprieve from parental responsibility, magnified into thinking that maybe it's not so smart to publicly discuss assassination dreams that could conceivably affect employment or harassment or who knows? Anyone who reads what I wrote knows I'm incapable on the level of simple logistics (can't imagine ever owning, let alone handling, a gun) but also too responsible for family and self to trade it in forever, none of which stops creeping paranoia from distracting me from an experience I paid too much for to stand too far from the stage.

No intricate execution-test songs, grooves and riffs, easier for them, only one song from my list of hope-to-hear songs, semi-disappointing but overall better than good. Too removed from the stage, distracted by chattering fans and the possibility of tumbling into someone rows below, even falling to death. Generally feeling blunted, ears fatigued as feet, too inside myself, un-bouncing, unlike a newborn elf.

During the climax of the second-to-last song of the second set—a rave-up improvised reprise of one of their most rocking early songs, albeit now with the drummer scatting "you get your ass handed to you every day," changing the emphasis with each pass through the phrase—I daydream about an ecstatic shitstorm (see "Inner Mission," page 75) and then, after a serviceable two-song encore, I sit on the edge of my raised seat, in no particular hurry to catch the train as I watch the arena empty.

Once the crowd's thinned down to a thousand stragglers, I see someone I know, a middle-aged bespectacled preppie Black guy, a good friend from college of a good high-school friend of mine, leaving his seat in the same section but on the lower level. I last saw him after a ten-mile run ten years ago. I left my apartment in South Philly after showering to get some Gatorade at CVS at the same exact time he got out of a car directly in front of my place and said goodbye to friends. He had an hour to kill before his ride back to New York arrived, suggested we get a beer, so we sat outside on East Passyunk Avenue near the dueling cheesesteakeries and had three before moving to Ray's Happy Birthday Bar for a fourth. We'd gone to Dead shows together at Giants Stadium with our mutual friend and had hung out in the early '90s, also at our mutual friend's bachelor party in 2002 or so. I told him I fell off the jam-band wagon long ago. He seemed disappointed, recommended Philadelphia's own Disco Biscuits, a band I'd never heard of.

Two years ago in April I saw him again at the memorial service for our mutual friend's father (a well-regarded Princeton economics professor). I wondered if I would see him again at the show, knowing he went to most Garden shows and had some connection to the band, once told me about hanging backstage with the guitarist's mother. And now I watched him on the lower level directly below where

I sat in the upper deck as he said goodbye to friends and slowly walked up his aisle toward the exit. I wasn't going to yell down to him, get his attention and wave. I suppose I could text him. He'd entered his number in my phone a decade ago and probably still has the same number. But by the time I turned my phone back on and sent something he'd be halfway out the arena. I was more interested in descending sidewinding escalators on sore feet and legs, satisfied but in no way energized like after shows by this or any other band that linger as "great."

Packed train home at 12:15, sandwich eaten watching the glowing new boarding display in Penn Station. A seat this time by the window. Young, vaguely Middle Eastern women in the vestibule car, lounging, leaning on each other. At a distance they seem flouncy and fashionable but they're shorter and younger when they eventually walk by. Awake enough, alone in a car now, and then walking wounded, dragging my weary shit-ass from the train to the parking lot, a tall woman in a white fur coat who resembles the writer from London walks behind me down the stairs. I find the car across an empty lot in a cluster of three cars still parked there.

Icy windshield, defroster all the way up, Dead station playing some mid-'70s rendition of "Big River." Empty highway except for distant headlights that come closer and closer and then cruise behind me too close if not quite tailgating. I hover between 50 and 55 MPH, accelerate to 60 MPH, hold my lane, aware of ice and deer, floating, and then an SUV police cruiser blows by and soon after exits toward Route 1.

Easy rest of the way home, I negotiate it all well enough, slip in at 2:22 am, eat half an English muffin with cheese and wasabi, get in bed, well-made and warm. Mom wakes up surprised I'm home already. Her big black Lab didn't even bark.

"The sea is not a mask."
—Wallace Stevens, *The Idea of Order at Key West*

ENCORE

BOY ... MAN ... GOD ... SHIT

A year after the passion week ending in Easter 2019, when we bought the new house and my father left home for good, every week we received messages from his facility about the number of residents and staff who'd tested positive and then the number of residents who'd died. It seemed inevitable that my father would get the virus, and then he tested positive, and a few days later they asked my mother to decide if my father should be taken to the hospital or transitioned to hospice care. The facility physician agreed with us that hospice care seemed like a better option, plus a nurse said he wasn't eating, hardly drinking, retaining fluid.

On a beautiful spring day, I sat in our backyard outside Philadelphia and talked to my mother in the Princeton area about what to do. She'd called a funeral home to arrange cremation. I was tasked with writing an obituary. We'd have a memorial once the pandemic was over. We essentially processed his death, Mamou joking about my father being "financially responsible to the end," unwilling to prolong his stay at a costly nursing home.

Every night that week dozens of satellites flew in a line an hour after sunset, like an artificial, well-organized meteor shower, something to turn heads to the skies after so long looking down into phones for updates on everything awful. Unlike all that hefty chaos on the surface of Earth, here was something meaningless, beautiful, apolitical, linear, simply good. Faint satellites skating across the night, one after another every twelve seconds or so, absolutely silent, barely visible, indisputably positive.

A year after the week my father nearly died, he's still with us yet diminished. Every Saturday afternoon my mother and I deploy high-tech devices to stream into his facility for a video session, each week repeating the same news about our move from Philadelphia, about Kali's age (she's eight now!), about why we appear as little rounded squares on a tablet screen, about how all this works. Every five minutes he turns the tablet to show us where he is, no idea what time it is, each week more confounded.

My father is still with us—for now, to a degree—but my mother's big black Lab had to be put down. Mamou was laid off with severance and then spent the year playing in the yard, supervising Chicken Free Time with Fluffbutt, Redneck, and Hen Solo, three chickens we rented and then adopted for good, building a teepee out of bamboo (bambeepee) and training honeysuckle and nasturtium to grow up it, and in September 2020 she helped Kali with school when it resumed online. I worked from home, thankful not to confront my colleague's desktop selections regarding George Floyd, the election, or the insurrection on January 6, 2021. I went to sleep same time as Kali before nine every night and woke at five to run nearly every morning, leaving the house before dawn, in August 2020 racking up an all-time monthly mileage high of a hundred-and-fifty miles, thinking it made sense to improve cardiovascular function and lose weight, especially as every profile I read of those lost to the virus seemed like they had underlying metabolic issues and insulin resistance. The original improvised draft of this story, thumbed on my phone from January through mid-March 2020 while taking the morning train, I let sit until after the election before editing it to seem composed like this, shaping raw disarray into something good I hope ("art is the triumph over chaos," per Cheever). Otherwise, without question, the established quarantine sheltering-in-place routine appeals to us, and now I worry about returning to the office, even if only once or twice a week, not to mention unbounded life in general.

Unable to tour, the band's guitarist and keyboardist released an album of old songs recorded as duets on the guitarist's porch overlooking evergreens and distant mountains. I laughed when the first track came on. The lyrics to "If I Could" still seem insipid when read online, but when sung by a pair of old friends I've known for decades, the performance reinforces the essential symbolic umbrella raised against precipitation in all its forms, including of course incessant celestial fecal matter.

The Path

A huge low sun bronzes the silent trees. Everything seems encased in autumn. The homes have settled into themselves, fifty years after construction. Kali will inherit the family home in fifty years if we're lucky. I will inherit the family home in twenty years, although few would call it lucky if my father makes it to ninety-five. My father and daughter are on opposite poles of their progression, one rising, one falling, one gaining knowledge, experience, speech, memory, the other losing everything other than an ever-increasing capacity to forget.

"Stay on the sidewalk," I say, holding her hand. "Concrete, not asphalt."

"Blacktop," she says, twisting my pinky finger. An animated movie starring a panda taught her to control me like this.

"No Wu-Shi fingerhold," I say.

"Yes Wu-Shi fingerhold," she says.

The panda executes the fingerhold at the end of the first installment of the trilogy, at the end of the third one, too, unleashing a shockwave that obliterates his opponent in the first one and sends his adversary to "the spirit realm" in the third one. The suggestion is clear: parents can be controlled with a twist of the pinky.

I say "run for me, run to that mailbox," and she says something about running toward a marathon, one apparently not far off right now.

"You run the marathon with me?" she says.

"I just ran one a few days ago," I say.

"You runned one?"

"*Ran*," I say. "I ran one."

The Sunday before Thanksgiving 2017 I had indeed *runned* one, or at least I started one and covered the miles on foot and completed one, running most of it, overwhelmed by wind gusts at times exceeding forty miles per hour. Hordes of thick brown sycamore leaves airborne all around plastered themselves to my neck, chest, thighs, shins. It was a good experience but I had wanted to finish in under five hours and make it at least twenty miles before walking a little. Instead, capacities blown by the wind, I integrated some walking into my lactic-acid impaired loping after sixteen miles. But at least I ran the last mile as hard as I could and finished strong, surprised by a cup of chicken broth I thought at first was mulled cider and by the appearance of wife and child. Mamou was somehow muddy. She had tripped and fallen while rushing to me and hurt her knee, so at the end of the marathon, after running and walking for almost six hours on a cold windy morning, I had to exert sympathy.

We shuffle along, my body recovered. I had planned to run for the first time since the marathon that morning but it was twenty-four degrees. It's warmed since then but it's still brisk.

"Run with me," she says, and we run the length of the Tucker's property, turning the soft rounded corner that descends toward the path, my daughter in no danger of toppling over, although I'm aware of every raised crack in the sidewalk ahead of her.

The Tucker's father was an alcoholic banker who regularly drank and drove, more often than not parking his car with at least one wheel on the curb. I only saw the mother when she emerged to check the mailbox at the end of their driveway. There was something of the rock star about their older son when he was a teenager. He had a Gibson Les Paul but couldn't really play it. He never left home and died from alcoholism by the time he was thirty. The younger son opened a bagel store, worked hard, drove a Corvette, and bought an apartment building in town. He may or may not still own the house.

"Look at that tree," I say, struck by an oak standing out from all the others in front of a house across the street. I had never seen it like this, had never noticed it. I had only ever stood on the house's porch on Halloween nearly forty years ago. The occupants were old then. Now and really forever they had always seemed nonexistent. To either side I know the houses better. In one lived a high-school girl-friend. She has a six-year-old daughter now and uses her neuroscience PhD at a major pharmaceutical company. In the other house was a friend who moved away before later attending Harvard and writing thrillers, but in that house I first played Pong—a plastic screen was taped to the TV so the little white blip produced by the primitive gaming console seemed like tennis.

"Look at how well the sun lights those leaves," I say.

"I like it. You buy it? You bought it?"

"It's not for sale, honey. You can just look at it for free."

It looks like a tree on the savannah, its leaves only accessible by giraffes. The trunk has turned a mottled white, like sickly duck plumage. As limbs fell except toward the top, the crusty red foliage assumed the shape of a cloud formation or maybe the hull of a ship.

I ask my daughter if the leaves look like a ship but she doesn't respond, distracted by purple berries on a shrub along the sidewalk, formerly the house of my mother's best friend, whose son now lives in Los Angeles and produces sit-coms for network television.

"Gentle," I say.

"I want them," she says, picking a few berries and bouncing them on her palm.

The berries are the purple that appears on insect wings, the crystalline iridescence apparent when enlarged in high-definition documentaries streamed to our home. I think of "Wooden Ships," a song I first heard on my Walkman while taking the dog around the same block thirty-two years ago. The line about eating purple berries for six or seven weeks without getting sick had seemed like hippie code for psychedelics. I now understand those berries as sustenance after the fall of civilization.

"Don't eat them, they could be poisonous," I say, also aware that the owner of the home could be watching from a window, upset that Kali picks their precious ornamental berries. "They're not Nerds," I say.

She dressed as a Power Ranger a few weeks ago and roamed city streets with me and her mother doing her best to demand treats, exposed for the first time as far as I know to the candy that comes in the form of tiny carbuncular nits of waxy sugar served in dual sectors of a perfect little bi-colored box. As she ate them at the kitchen table, a huge bowl filled with her booty, the influx of sugar seemed like a rite of passage, like the host, the body of the country, exciting, artificial, mass-produced, enticing, unnaturally sweet, momentarily delectable but deleterious in the end. I knocked the berries out of her hand and directed her down the sidewalk toward the path.

"You see that cat?"

"Two of them, two catties," she says, and she's right. Two cats roam the neighborhood, or at least their yards, unlike our housecats, one of which has stopped using the litter box, depositing shit in the middle of the kitchen, in the same spot each time. Every morning there's a new turd. Every time we come home from work and pre-school one of our cats has issued a fresh criticism of the quality of our care and affection for them. I bet it's the beautiful snow-white neurotic asocial cat that does it, the one that only emerges to hump my wife and then fellate itself, the one I always say that could be magically removed from our household and at most I would say "oh." In exchange for my apathy, I receive small dry turds in the morning and evening, a consistent cycle integrated into the pattern of our lives. Maybe I should change the litter more often.

Every morning she says she wants a dog, *needs* a dog. Exploratory questions regarding what she may want from Santa yield responses related to a small canine. The cats at home are valuable in that they preclude the arrival of a dog, plus we would need to hire a daytime dog walker to take it around every day while we're at work, our child and pets unseen except mornings, nights, and weekends, our real weekday work-hour life somewhere other than home. I suppose that division, that distance between the realities of work and the ideal of home, includes the benefit of stability and keeps us from becoming overexposed to one another. Without separation daily, my daughter would not gallop into my arms when I pick her up from pre-school. The joy of coming back together daily in the early evening is a benefit, too. Every day, more or less, with some variations, we're on our established courses throughout the world, Kali in one place, Mamou and I on the move, negotiating the cycles of our days, always in tandem yet so often apart.

"Shoulders," she says, mispronouncing it a little, the way she mispronounces everything.

"Shoulders," I say, mocking her, my eyes as needy as hers, my skin momentarily as clear and pure, my hair as thick and rich and free of gray.

In response she stands in front of me, back to me, arms raised enough to offer access to her ribs for easy uplift. My only real insight into humanity now that I'm a parent is that our torsos are ribbed for flexible protection of internal organs but also, like the laces on a football, to help parents grip children better, to levitate them, like the gods who brought them into existence, into the air. As always, whenever she presents herself for liftoff to my shoulders, I try to climb aboard, hooking one leg over her, straddling her head, which she always finds hilarious, an image I love too, a fifty-pound girl carrying her two-hundred plus father on her shoulders. When I have her on my shoulders as we walk home down a city street, I see our reflection in shop windows, eight feet tall, indomitable yet endangered, unvanquishable yet liable to collapse, which feels absolutely and definitively beautiful.

"Let's cross," I say.

"Asphalt," she says and reaches for my hand, trained that blacktop means street means hold hands, whereas on the concrete she can roam free if she doesn't run.

We make it across the street to the concrete sidewalk in front of a house I can't remember being in, only hearing that its owner at the time invented the mechanism by which a plastic bottle when squeezed would elevate the correct dosage of mouthwash to the protected area under the cap. A rumor of widespread international impact originating at the local level emitted a sense that the enclosed area of youth was the center of the world, or at least *significant* in some way.

The roof of the next house every Christmastime hosted Santa and reindeer in flight, plastic and illuminated, although it doesn't seem like anyone lives there now, accumulated leaves on the front porch, fallen tree limbs, the Plexiglas basketball backboard in the driveway stained opaque. I don't remember ever seeing anyone there, gardening, parking a car, not even a light in a window, the mysterious house at the bottom of a slight hill where the road comes around and, at that point, the path originates between our neighborhood and the old streets of the village.

The path, a narrow strip of pavement no longer than half a football field, on one side is bordered by a chain-link fence covered in honeysuckle, dense, fragrant, and when manipulated by knowledgeable, slightly older, expert fingertips yields a jewel of nectar atop the filament within the white flower, a pearl sweet more by sight than taste, a substance insufficient in quantity that nourishes if savored at the right age, wholly fulfilling in quality. My daughter is too young for honeysuckle, plus it's November. No flowers or filaments reveal perfect little drops of nectar.

"One day I'll teach you how to get honey from the flowers here," I say. "And down here by the creek, Daddy spent a lot of time when he was a little older than you, catching water spiders and salamanders and . . ."

"Salamanders?"

"Little amphibious lizards. *Amphibious* means they can live in water and on land like us. They're amphibians."

"I'm amphilabians," she says.

I don't tell her about how we called the path "The Runway" when we were teenagers, how we went there and stood midway down it, protected by the thickest shrubs, and packed bowls with skunk, sense, or schwag, how "The

Runway" became the sight of an infamous night in my friendship with Crow when I flicked a lighter's flame at his bangs in response to something he'd said and they ignited thanks to hairspray I didn't know he'd used, his scalp burning blue and bright in the darkest spot along the path, at one of the most primordial, unenlightened times of our lives, although who can really remember or judge, being amphibians at the time ourselves, half-adult, half-child, expected to swim despite doubts about staying afloat.

"The Path," the least pretentious name for it possible, assumed the somewhat more evocative "The Runway" for only a few years, after which it reverted to "The Path," only called "The Runway" in reference to those nights we'd stopped to avail ourselves of the darkness. I can't picture my child smoking there in ten years, just ten years from now, my parents midway into their eighties, maybe able-bodied, my father's memory fading fast, my daughter's memory of the path as a child similar to mine, minus the time we found a Japanese pornographic cartoon book in the creek, dried it out, and puzzled over the images.

"Oh, it's dry, Honey. No water spiders today."

She doesn't seem too disappointed not to find water flowing over the rocks below the little paved bridge over the creek. A wooden fence keeps her from the few-foot plummet into the dry stones, identical polygons, most likely purchased in bulk and placed there by the township, not irregular shapes, sometimes smooth and circular or ovular or triangular and pointed, the sort that once were offered to me as arrowheads in exchange for my precious collection of feathers, when I learned an early lesson about trading with older kids. I've never considered the long-term impact on my character of being duped like that early in life. My parents' reaction was that I had made the trade so I had to live with it. I could always start a new feather collection and maybe one of the arrowheads was really an arrowhead. We could take them to the museum in Trenton for verification. At that time in my life, pheasant feathers and arrowheads were the holiest objects, grails I hoped to discover in woods that would be cut down for a new development in less than a decade.

At the end of the path, she again wants me to carry her and I raise her and cradle her legs in my right arm, so our faces can be close, cheek to cheek. She loves the view.

"You'll be tall like this one day," I tell her, the same as I always do when she's close enough I can whisper as I relieve her feet for a block or two on the mile walk to and from pre-school. "You'll be tall like me, taller than most, like a god." I don't mean omnipotent, I just mean she'll have a good view, if not an all-seeing one or anything all that special, really, but then, there, cheek to cheek like that, the elevation seems divine.

I carry her for twenty feet along one of the four old streets of the town, straight shots a third of a mile between the old Prep School's campus and what used to be the edge of the woods and the farm beyond it, each now settled into their current forms of homes from Toll Brothers worth four-hundred thousand dollars or more, every third model more or less the same. I deposit her after a short carry on the old railroad tracks, which had heavy splintered wooden ties and where rusty iron spikes could be found and brought home and traded for baseball cards and feathers. It always seemed dangerous playing around the old railroad tracks, as though the train would come to life and rush down it, crushing us beneath furious ghost wheels. Or maybe the older kids, Tucker, Pillon, their surnames like Old West gunslinger villains, would get us.

Pillon had dug a pit near where the railroad tracks crossed the creek, put a roof on it of old linoleum, and created a little insidious world down there that scared kids my age more than anything in movies or books. He was fifteen or sixteen, probably a poor student, maybe with a learning disability, maybe with parents who drank, maybe living beyond their means more than most in the neighborhood where money never seemed an issue but also was never flaunted. Pillon probably smoked pot in his pit. Drank. Maybe masturbated to the porn we sometimes discovered. But this was before they developed the pine and bamboo over by the creek along the old tracks, where there's now a nice house, a cul de sac of modern designs, each unique, lots of angles and light, wooded yards with vibrant green grass, unnatural for November it seems.

The old house through a stand of trees along the former railroad tracks, the kid who lived there fell down dead in his twenties while training for the New York City marathon. Heart condition. Gone. Just like that. Twenty years ago or so.

"See those little rocks, Honey. They're called gravel."

She picks up a handful, studies it, sifts it through her fingers, picks up another little pile and says she'll put it in her pocket to bring to Grandpa's house. She refers to my mother as Grandpa, sensing I think that my mother runs the household, is the so-called man of the house, my father now diminished, frazzle-haired, always cold.

I've stopped worrying about gravel in her pockets. There's no way to stop it. I walk ahead and the sun is low and behind me when I turn to coax her to *come on*. Amber light, the leaves red, brown, some eerily green, the sky blue, deeply so, cloudless, everything fresh like a rainstorm had come through and passed but the ground isn't wet. It's just gorgeous, super-autumnal, radiant, approaching the edge of winter but not there yet.

I manage to get her to follow me, to move on, about to where Pillon once had his pit, his underground fort about forty years ago now, somehow. The newer houses to the left along the gravel path, along the old railroad tracks, glisten in the light, and in the driveway of one is a large dog, standing at attention, ears up, tail alert, a wolf-white German Shepherd, not yet barking, aware of us.

"Look at the doggie," I say. "It sees us. We might have to run."

The dog barks and I say "run, run," and she says "run a marathon," associating running in any form with the unnaturally long run I completed the previous weekend, disappointed in my performance on race day but grateful for being able to complete the training without injury, for sticking with it, increasing mileage each month until every Sunday morning up at five and out the door by six, the full October moon hanging above, the winter constellation Orion seen again as I stepped outside, covering the same ground through the city to the loop along the river, each run another mile more, until I had to switch the route to lengthen it to a twenty-mile loop, repeating it on consecutive weekends, able to do it, strong despite the disappointing final run when it counted, like preparations for a wedding disrupted by winds that send flowers and decorations and guests scurrying for cover, not a disaster, not a tornado obliterating everything, but enough of a disturbance to undermine the vision held for so long of a good day.

"Run, baby, run, he's coming after us," I say, and she runs ahead, still saying something about the marathon, as the dog stays put, not coming after us, just one of the little lies I deploy to move her along when going to and from school or the park.

I peek over the fence at the old neighborhood swim club, a pool surrounded by woods, always buggy and filled with leaves when I was there once or twice as a kid, but it's still there and the same. With the water half drained reflecting the sky and leaves everywhere it's worth a photo, so I flip up the screen of my phone and take some, not sure how good they are, and then I lift my child so she can see what I see. I put her down again and look at the photos, thinking one better than the others. I post it to Instagram after fussing with it a little but then delete it, something's off, the picture doesn't capture the day, and by the time I emerge from this reverie, my daughter has returned to the gravel path and now sees a man coming, walking a little doggie. The white dog could have attacked as I fussed with my phone, engaging with the few hundred people I follow and who follow me, instead of following and leading my child on this radiant walk.

Every dog we see she wants to pet but not every dog likes to be petted. The man now walking the dog seems like he's had some early Thanksgiving wine, not drunk but not sober either, not dressed to encounter strangers. There's something about his manner that reminds me of when I pop out on a weekend morning to the store a block away wearing sweatpants and sweatshirt and flip flops and see someone I know, like it's been a private day for him that our presence on the old railroad tracks makes public.

"He's missing a leg," the man says, and it's clear that the lower part of the dog's back right leg is missing. "He's a rescue, walking him for a friend," he says, not that we were wondering if this gimpy Chihuahua pug mix were his dog or not.

I restrain my daughter, who always seems so fascinated by dogs, maybe because they're often smaller than she is and are led around on leashes, the way not so long ago we strapped her into a stroller so we could walk somewhere without her sitting on every stoop or running toward traffic. Sometimes she pretends to take me for a walk, like I'm my mother's enormous Lab mix, now on his last legs but once he stood tall and proud, the first dog I've ever seen that seemed to have six-pack abs visible through its belly fur, so well trained, from a military family in Tennessee. My mother's dog has lately become obscenely flatulent, almost didn't make it through the summer, alive only because my mother shows him mercy and wants him to have another day sitting in the sun, day after day, the decision to put the old dog down more poignant the older my parents get, the parallel all too clear.

My shadow now seems excessively long, in a long black coat, holding the stick my child handed me so we could have a swordfight. I raise it and I look like the Hermit in the Tarot, or the Grim Reaper. With shadow cast by long coat and arm raised, there's something mythic about it.

"Look at my shadow, Honey," I say.

She tries to swordfight with my shadow, which parries and thrusts as I say "on guard" and "touché" as always during swordfights. Her best chance to win a college scholarship will be either crew or fencing, we always say, aware she might not have the coordination to excel at standard sports but may need sports to help her candidacy, or maybe she won't even bother with college. A year and a half behind her classmates now, maybe she'll catch them. She seems to know more than she lets on, surprising us with vocabulary, memory, humor, more and more. Day by day, week by week, the cycle of walks to and from school, weekend excursions to the nature preserve, daily sessions with therapists at pre-school, straightens and accelerates a slow undulation of progress. When she's twenty-six no one will say she seems twenty four and a half.

I take out my phone and capture some images I don't post. Instead I start a "story" on Instagram, a short video on

which, as though she knows I'm filming, she yells MAGIC
WIZARD DISAPPEAR, muttering in her little child's voice
"oh that didn't work" before rushing me at close range
with her stick pointed at my thigh. I send the video and
it's temporarily accessible around the world, will be seen
by ten percent of my friends on there, twenty-five people, the image's significance quantified by exposure, before
it disappears forever. I traditionally upload a still image,
too, something she'll always she if I ever follow through
and print Instagram posts via the photo-publishing service
Mamou purchased for me last Christmas or birthday but I
can never remember to create, these little bound paperback
collections of images reminiscent of old-fashioned photo
albums, the thick spiral-bound sort spread open with left
and right covers on adjoining right and left thighs of one
person taking another on a tour of glossy, rectangular, pho-
tographic memories.

We now return to the neighborhood proper, taking a
short path past a screened-in porch where I first saw a
horseshoe crab shell, maybe thirty-five years ago. The boy
who lived there was hit in the face with a baseball bat, the
barrel swung back into him as he played catcher, a street
game, blood everywhere, parents emerged from houses
with towels to take him to the hospital. The eldest daughter was the first to stir my loins when I was six or seven
and she was in her teens. I wanted to tell her at the time
but embarrassment got the better of me and I kept the phe-
nomenon to myself. At the bottom of a slight hill, enough
to skateboard down and get some speed, the kids who lived

over here were sassier than those who lived at the top of the hill and around the corner, their parents were younger and one of their mothers was French and wore a tube top. Now I negotiate my daughter across the street, up the hill, back to my parents' house. The leaves are mostly down and swept away. I used to like how the streets narrowed with piles of leaves and then widened again once collected, the banks of the streets along the curbs slick with greasy organic residue.

"Oh, look, a plane. You see it?"

"Take us on a trip?" she says.

"It's just a little plane. I've never seen one so low here."

It flies in loose circles over the neighborhood, like a mechanical vulture, the same blue as the sky. The engine sounds like lawnmowers at work in the summer, but now it's otherwise silent, and with the sun low and the trees skeletal, the plane's trajectory in eccentric circles can be seen clearly, how it rises and falls, climbs and glides, the pilot's head almost apparent but it's a projection at best, goggles, leather cap, scarf, a dog-fighter taking on the Red Baron.

"Wave at the plane," I say, and she waves and jumps a quarter inch off the ground as the plane passes overhead. I imagine it strafing us with machine gun fire, the yards turning over with the rain of bullets, my daughter and I taking cover in a pile of leaves or in the open garage of the house of the first and to this day only Black family in the neighborhood. The older of the two boys I grew up with sang for a popular cover band that played packed bars at the shore in the summer. The younger brother moved to California and now has a blond daughter, or so it seems on social media.

I extract my phone and upload live video of the plane circling but when I look at the videos immediately after uploading them I delete them because they don't capture the effect of the sun, the rare sight of a blue plane turning scavenger circles in a clear sky, the radiance of it, what it must be like from the pilot's perspective, the view, the layout, the predominance of trees, the carefree exuberance of circling like this, covering the same tract of aerial space, around and around to the point that I expect to see crop circles above, ribbons of exhaust and vapor forming a ring above us, like skywriting delivering a cryptic statement on behalf of celestial sponsors.

The former pitcher for the Philadelphia Phillies who threw a no-hitter in the World Series and a perfect game, a gunslinger with a name to match, Roy Halladay, crashed a small aircraft into the water off the coast of Florida, rising high and then dive-bombing and skimming the water until he was dead at forty, somehow five years younger than I am, although he was always older as a star pitcher, retired and waiting his turn for induction into the Hall of Fame. In April, the estranged wife of a good college friend of my wife's, an attendee at our wedding, was flying with her two young sons in a small plane piloted by her new boyfriend when they went down into the Caribbean en route to Miami from Bermuda.

I watch the plane come around really low again over the houses to the west, the sun behind it, and see it come around and climb again, wanting it to take another loop and descend at maximum speed, not into my parents' house or the house of a neighbor as stunned Thanksgiving guests exit their cars after long drives. Instead I want it to descend with grace and care and land along the stretch of relatively level and wide asphalt in front of my parents' home. I want the pilot to emerge, give my daughter a Thanksgiving gift, an outdated analogue device for orientation (map, compass), and then as we wave *bye bye* I want the plane to ascend and disappear over the housing developments that used to be woods and farms as we spend what's left of the day in quiet gratitude.

Lee Klein is the author of *Neutral Evil)))* (Sagging Meniscus), *JRZDVLZ* (Sagging Meniscus), *The Shimmering Go-Between* (Atticus Books) and *Thanks + Sorry + Good Luck: Rejection Letters from the Eyeshot Outbox* (Barrelhouse Books), and translator of Horacio Castellanos Moya's *Revulsion: Thomas Bernhard in San Salvador* (New Directions), for which he received a 2015 PEN/Heim Translation Fund Award. He lives in the Philadelphia area with his wife and daughter. Visit litfunforever.com for more.